Joshua's Stable

Cathal O'Toole

BALBOA
PRESS
A DIVISION OF HAY HOUSE

Balboa Press books may be ordered through booksellers or by contacting:

Balboa Press
A Division of Hay House
1663 Liberty Drive
Bloomington, IN 47403
www.balboapress.com
1-(877) 407-4847

ISBN: 978-1-4525-3799-3 (sc)
ISBN: 978-1-4525-3800-6 (e)

Printed in the United States of America

Balboa Press rev. date: 8/26/2011

CONTENTS

To my wife, soul-mate and best friend, Susan Elizabeth, for your patience, wisdom and help in writing this book.

Acknowledgements

When I was very young my father built a beautiful Nativity scene within a large cardboard box. He cut out a perfect star above the door lintel, and with frosted glass and a light bulb, the effect was magical. It appeared as though the star was lighting up the whole stable, as it shone on the straw, the animals and the whole manger scene.

My summer holidays as a young boy, were spent on my uncles farm in rural Ireland. There was no electricity or running water and we had to make trips with the horse and cart to fetch water from the village well. We also visited the local blacksmith to watch the horse being shod. These memories, over the years led me to write the story of "Joshua's Stable".

I would like to thank my dear wife, Susan, for her help with the story line, typing and editing and her patience with me. My children Judith, Jennie, Katie and Ryan also helped me a great deal in the first drafts of this book.

Chapter 1

Joshua lay in his bed gazing at the ceiling. He was suddenly filled with sadness at the realization that, after tonight, he would never see his home again. He had lived all his life in this little house in Rimmon, a tiny hamlet not far from Bethlehem. He remembered waking to the smell of his mother's baking, as he lay in bed with the sun streaming in and the birds chirping. He awoke excited at the prospect of helping his father in the great shed at the back of the house. Even at four years old, Joshua would leap out of bed, charge into the kitchen, and grab a hunk of his mother's fresh baked bread. Taking a swig from the pitcher of goat's milk on the table and shouting "Hi Mama," he ran out the door to help light the fire in the big shed for his father.

Joshua's father was the village blacksmith. Joshua adored the big man and marveled at how his father could swing the huge hammer while holding a red-hot horseshoe with pincers over the anvil.

"One day," he used to think, "I will be able to do that just like my father."

From a very early age, Mark Ben-Gideon had taught and encouraged his little boy in all the tasks of the blacksmiths trade. The big fire would be lit first thing in the morning. By the time he was five, Joshua was able to light the fire all by himself. Then his father would come into the shed.

"I don't believe it," the blacksmith always said. "How on earth did that fire get lit?" Joshua would laugh delightedly

"I did it myself Daddy."

Then the big man whooped with delight. Laughing he scooped young Joshua into the air and set him on his shoulders. They made their

1

way down the meadow at the back of their house to the little stream where they would strip off their tunics and bathe in the cold spring water. Mark then led his son to a large tree nearby and they put their tunics back on and knelt in prayer.

From the time Joshua was very little, his father had taught him about God. He always told his son that he believed it was very important to talk to God every morning after bathing. He used to tell Joshua how God has made this beautiful world for our pleasure and that He loves to hear us give Him thanks and praise.

"If we don't thank Him for all He has given us Joshua," Mark explained, "then how can we ask His help when things go terribly wrong?"

Joshua also remembered another favorite saying of his father's.

"People always ask God for what they want, but we should be asking our Heavenly Father what it is that He wants from us."

The blacksmith told his son that in listening to God, we had to become very quiet and still in our mind. That's how we heard God speaking to us.

"Sometimes," he said, "you can actually hear Him speak but mostly you just feel His warm loving presence beside you."

Joshua loved these early mornings at the stream and under the big tree in quiet prayer with his father and God. He actually felt God's warm and loving presence and was always a little sad when it was time to rise and walk back to the blacksmith's shed. Joshua went straight to the big bellows that were used to puff air on the fire and make its flames roar higher.

The Roman army had a garrison of legionaries a few miles away and these legionaries were Mark's biggest customers. It was not unusual for a couple of legionaries to be waiting on horseback outside the shed when they got back from the stream. For the most part the Roman soldiers were polite. Many could not speak Hebrew and communicated by sign language. Over time, both Joshua and his father learned many Latin words and were able to speak with their customers.

"One thing about the Romans," Mark Ben-Gideon said, "they always pay for my services and never owe me money."

With all the business that came from the Romans, the blacksmith nearly always had a surplus of money at the end of each week. Every few days he would move the heavy anvil, underneath which was a small wooden trapdoor. Under the trapdoor was a small hole containing a large earthen jar and into this jar, he would place the surplus coins he had earned. One day Joshua asked him why he was saving all this money.

"Well Joshua," he replied, "every six months we travel to Bethlehem to buy supplies for the business. The remainder of the savings will go to helping your mother and me, when I get too old to work".

"But Papa I will work and run the business when you are old and I will take care of you and Mama," Joshua said laughing. Little did the boy know as he spoke those words that in the coming years he would lose both his parents . . .

Chapter 2

A few short months after Joshua turned fourteen, his father had a terrible accident. A horse he was shoeing for a Roman centurion got startled and kicked the blacksmith, knocking him into the fire. His head crashed into the large funnel chimney over the fire pit and for a few seconds he lay unconscious in the roaring flames until Joshua and the centurion pulled him out. They frantically beat out the flames on his burning tunic, then carried him into the house and laid him down on his bed. Joshua's mother, Dinah, wept and knelt beside her husband holding his hand. The skin on the side of his face, his arm and upper body were all very badly burned. Joshua could hardly see anything through the tears streaming down his face. He knew his father was in agony

The centurion gently led Joshua's mother to the other side of the room. He told her to pour a pitcher of cold water gently over the burns and then to cover the burns with palm fronds and place cold mud packs on top. "But I must tell you" he added. "With burns as bad as these he will probably not last the night."

On hearing, this Joshua began wailing. "Noooooo, he cried, "nooooo . . ." We have to get that healing man who lives in Cana, Eli "The centurion shook his head and placed his hand on Joshua's shoulder." Eli is very good at helping people with fevers or sprained ankles," he said, "but your father's injuries are far more serious. You must pray."

He then handed a large bag of coins to Joshua's mother. "This is for your husband's services to my horse. I hope he will recover. I will pray for you all." With that, he walked out the door.

Joshua had never been so scared in all his life. Seeing his father, this great big, warm, loving man lying there moaning and gasping for air, half his face burnt away, was more than he and his mother could bear. They sank to their knees on either side of him and cried while holding his hands.

"What can we do Mama?"

"Maybe we should go and get Magda," she said.

Magda was the hamlet's wise old lady. Some said she was a healer and that she could see into the future. She was often on hand to help with childbirth and would also come to people's homes when someone had died, to lay them out in preparation for burial.

"No Mama," he shouted, "she comes for dead people.

Joshua's mother gently explained that Magda was also very good at helping sick people. The blacksmith seemed to be nodding his head between moans and gasps and trying to mumble something. Joshua put his ear to his father's lips to hear what he was trying to say.

"I think he wants some water Mama".

She went and got a goblet with some water and together, gently holding his head they poured a few drops on his parched lips. Suddenly the big man began to shake violently.

"Run quickly and get Magda," said Joshua's mother.

Joshua raced out of the house and down the hill to the little hamlet of Rimmon. He could hardly see for the tears streaming down his face. When he reached Magda's house he burst in through her door without knocking. Magda was lifting a pail of water near her fire and looked up in surprise at her tear-stained visitor.

"Come quickly Magda. My father's been very badly burnt in an accident and we need you."

Without saying a word, Magda dried her hands on her apron and followed Joshua back to his house.

On seeing the blacksmith's injuries, she just shook her head and began to chant a psalm to God . . . Joshua who had heard the same psalm chanted at funerals sobbed, "Noooooo"

Magda gently led him outside. She explained that God would not want this wonderful man to suffer for a long time. She said that God was calling him home and that Joshua must pray that his father's death would not be a long painful one. Joshua just sobbed

"I will hate God forever if He takes my father away."

Magda tried to reason with the boy but he could not be consoled.

For three days and three nights, Joshua and his mother ministered to the blacksmith, never leaving his side. On the fourth morning after the accident, he died.

Mark Ben-Gideon was buried in a little plot at the rear of his blacksmith's shed while most of the villagers looked on and Rabbi Gershing chanted and said prayers. Joshua, numb with grief, was oblivious to everything.

Chapter 3

For three weeks after his father's death Joshua and his mother cried themselves to sleep every night and awoke every morning to a deep sadness. In the first weeks, after the funeral, neighbors kept coming with baked goods and meals. The food kept piling up but neither Joshua nor his mother had any appetite and most of it ended up being fed to animals. As the villagers noticed that their food was not being eaten they gradually stopped bringing foodstuffs. Then came the day when no one visited the home except for two Roman legionaries who wanted their horses shod. Joshua tried not to cry as he explained to them that his father had died. However, as he said this, big tears rolled down his cheek.

"So," said one of the legionaries, "will you be getting anyone to run your business? You know your father was the only blacksmith for miles around."

Joshua told them he did not know and the Romans rode off. Then he went into his house and sat down beside his mother at the table. He told her what the soldiers had said.

"What are we going to do Joshua? We have no money and your father is gone. What are we going to do?" She started to cry. Joshua had never seen his mother look so helpless.

"But Mama, we have money". He said, running and retrieving the pouch of money the centurion had given to them. He counted out the large pile of coins. It was about six times what his father would have charged the soldier for shoeing a horse. It was a large sum of money. Joshua's mother's eyes opened wide in astonishment at such a large pile of coins.

"What a kind man that Roman is" she said, but after a moment, tears came back to her eyes.

"This will only last us a few weeks if we are very careful, and then what will we do?"

Joshua suddenly felt very grown up.

"We shall hire a strong young man to forge the shoes. I will train him myself" Joshua's mother smiled as she watched her young son's effort to solve the family's problem. She saw the quiet determination that she had seen so often in her husband's eyes and she knew that if anyone could do this, Joshua could.

They started talking about all the young men in the village who might be able and willing to learn the blacksmith's trade. After discussing many of the younger men who lived in the village, they were left with two choices. Joshua favored Uri who was twenty-two. Uri had been run over by a Roman chariot when he was a little boy. He had suffered a broken nose, a scarred face and a broken leg. His leg had healed badly in a crooked way and he now walked with a peculiar gait, dragging his bad leg behind him. His twisted nose and scarred cheek made him look as though he was grinning madly at everyone all the time. However, Joshua knew him to be a hard worker who had on occasion helped the village carpenter. He had once helped Ben-Gideon to move some heavy equipment in the shed. Joshua liked the young man even though many villagers made fun of his grinning face and crooked walk.

Seth, on the other hand was a handsome, twenty year old who lived with his widowed mother and, from what Joshua had heard, he liked to party with some rough company and was frequently drunk. Joshua did not know him very well but had a strong instinctive dislike for him. When his mother asked him why this was, he thought for a moment before replying.

"I'm not sure. I hear he drinks a lot."

"That's not a very good reason Joshua, the man is strong and healthy and his appearance is nice."

What she was really saying was that Uri might frighten away customers with his maniacal grin and crooked walk. Joshua looked up at his mother and saw the determined look in her eye. She wanted to employ Seth. He knew it would be useless to argue with her. He got up and went down the meadow to the stream

He took off his tunic and began to bathe. Looking up at the large tree, he felt a strong desire to go, kneel, and ask God's help. Should they should employ Seth or not? However, fond memories of his early morning meditations and prayers with his father came into his mind and he felt an enormous sense of loss and hurt about his father's death. Why had God taken his great, big, loving father away? Joshua felt angry, hurt and betrayed by his God. He turned his back on the large tree.

"God", he said, "I do not want to talk to You".

"But I am here Joshua and I will always be with you."

The pull was very strong and Joshua almost turned around, but then anger and hurt boiled up inside him and he gritted his teeth.

"I don't want to talk to you. You took my father."

He jumped out of the stream, snatched up his tunic and hurried up the meadow to his house. As he entered, his mother was seated at the table with her hands in a bowl. She looked up as he came in.

"Have you been?" she asked.

"Been where?"

"To see Seth of course."

Joshua suddenly became aware that his mother had changed out of her mourning clothes. She had donned fresh clothes and had done something different with her hair. She looked younger and prettier.

"You look good Mama."

"Have you been to talk to Seth?"

"Oh, uh, no. I just went for a bathe in the stream. I'll go and see him now."

Chapter 4

The next day, late in the morning, Seth was at the anvil. He was swinging the heavy hammer and trying to forge the red-hot horseshoe he was holding with pincers in his other hand over the anvil. He was a big and brawny young man. Although he had plenty of strength, he had very poor coordination and could not seem to hit the horseshoe with the heavy hammer. Joshua tried to show him and encourage him but Seth just became more and more frustrated and angry. He cursed every time he missed with the hammer and eventually he flung the hammer away in disgust and stormed out of the shed.

Although Joshua was tempted to run after him and beg him to come back and try again, as he thought about how the morning had gone, he decided against it. Seth had arrived much later than he had agreed to the previous day. He had swaggered into the shed with an air of arrogance. He seemed to resent Joshua's attempts to teach him anything. He had made many demeaning comments, about the sheds untidiness, about how old the tools were and how the fire was not hot enough. He acted as though he owned the blacksmith's forge and knew everything there was to know about it. As Joshua reflected on the morning, he said aloud "We don't need him. I can do this myself"

Taking the hammer in his hands, he began practicing swinging it, as he had watched his father do many times. He swung it high above his head and down to an exact spot on the anvil. Time and time again, he practiced until sweat rolled down his forehead into his eyes. The muscles in his back and shoulders screamed with pain. After about an hour, he felt as though he was getting the hang of it. His legs were trembling with fatigue but he felt with more practice tomorrow and the next day that he, Joshua Ben-Gideon, would be able to forge horseshoes and run the blacksmithing business just like his father had done. After all, he already knew how to use the small hammer and was adept at forging small tools like scythes for farmers and spears and arrowheads. The most important part of the business was shoeing horses for the Romans. If they could not get their horses shod here then they would take their business elsewhere. Joshua knew he would not allow that to happen. He tidied up the shed and put everything away. Feeling very proud of himself, he doused the fire and trudged back to his house.

As he approached the house, he thought he heard his mother laughing. He opened the door and was amazed to see his mother seated at the table with Seth and a half carafe of wine. They were both drinking and laughing. His mother looked at Joshua, her eyes sparkling

"Seth says that father's tools are old fashioned and out of date. He is going to try and get us some new tools. He believes he can take over the business and run it for us. Isn't that great Joshua?"

Joshua was speechless. Seth who could not even swing a heavy hammer properly, who knew nothing about forging tools or horseshoes, was trying to tell them that his father's tools were no good! Joshua felt his legs go weak. He collapsed on the remaining stool.

"Have some wine Josh," Seth said pushing a goblet towards him.

"My name is Joshua not Josh and I don't want any wine," Joshua yelled, banging his fist down on the table. Then with tears streaming down his face, he ran out of the house. As he reached the door, he heard his mother saying "He's still very upset and missing his father".

He wanted to scream at her, "I'm very upset at Seth for thinking he can run our business." but instead, he ran all the way down to the stream and threw his tunic off. He began rubbing water all over his body. Then he cupped his hands and drank from the cool stream water. He felt like he might explode . . . Memories of his father taking him in his arms when he was little came back to him. He remembered his father's words:

"Now let's listen to what God is telling us. Whenever we get really mad or upset Joshua, God is standing right behind us waiting to tell us something great. So now Joshua, listen to God to help us find what is great about this situation."

11

On every occasion when Joshua became angry, his father had patiently gone through the same ritual. It had become such habit over the years that Joshua now once again found himself again going towards the large tree where they had always prayed. But his terrible grief at the loss of his father and his feelings of hurt and betrayal by God overcame him again and he turned his back on the tree. He kicked at a stick that was lying on the ground, but kicking hurt his foot and did not help his mood. Once again, tears rolled down his cheeks. What was he going to do? He sat down, put his head in his hands, and tried to think. Maybe when Seth had gone for the night he would be able to talk to his mother and tell her exactly what Seth was like, how little he really knew, and unable he was to use the heavy hammer and forge horseshoes. With a little more practice, Joshua himself would be able to forge horseshoes just as his father had.

He would however need some assistance. He would probably need someone a lot bigger than himself to deal with Roman legionaries and local farmers. The thought of working with Seth was revolting. He remembered his mother and Seth laughing and drinking together. He felt upset with his mother for making him hire Seth. He was also angry that she and Seth could laugh so soon after his father's death. To Joshua, whose pain and sense of loss was so deep, it seemed like yesterday that his father had died.

If only there was someone, to whom he could talk. Mark Ben-Gideon had been an only child and both of his parents, Joshua's grandparents, had died many years ago. There was an aunt, Shalom who was his mother's sister. She had visited once but now lived many miles away. It was then he thought of Magda, the old widow who had helped when his father was dying and who laid out Ben-Gideon's body for burial. She seemed to be a very stern old woman but her eyes shone with a bright twinkle and a deep wisdom. Rumor had it that she had the gift of prophesy and could tell people's futures. She had a certain presence and wisdom that seemed very comforting to Joshua. Feeling a sudden urge to go and visit with her, he put his tunic on and walked up the meadow and then down the track into the little hamlet of Rimmon.

Chapter 5

Magda's house lay at the other end of the hamlet. As he approached the door, it opened and Magda stood there, a bright twinkle in her eye.

"Come in young Joshua. I've been expecting you."

"Ex—expecting me?" he stammered. After all, he hardly knew this woman.

"Yes. I got to thinking about you and your Mama. Then I prayed for both of you and then God asked me to talk to you." She said this in a very matter—of—fact tone . . . Joshua just nodded his head, his mouth agape.

"Seth is going to be a whole heap of trouble for you and your Mama."

How did you know about Seth?"

She turned and walked back into her house and bent over a big tub full of soaking clothes and began prodding it with a big stick. She had been in the middle of doing some villagers laundry before Joshua arrived.

There's very little that goes on round here that old Magda doesn't know about," she said, her eyes twinkling. "But I'm afraid, young man that you will have to put up with Seth for a few weeks."

Joshua found himself very much in awe of this old woman. Her intense blue eyes seemed to see right into his very soul.

Why is that?" he asked.

Because" she said with a big sigh, "it is God's will".

Tears started rolling down his face as he remembered how God had betrayed him and left him fatherless. Magda looked at him intently.

"Joshua, God loves you dearly, so much so that he has a very special task for you and only you." She paused a moment and looked up at the ceiling. "This special task will bring you great joy and blessings and great honor to your parents. But I have to tell you that the next few weeks will be ones of trouble and hardship for you and your mother. But be of good cheer. When these weeks of heartbreak are over you will find a joy and a peace such as is rarely found in this world." She was silent for a few moments as Joshua digested what she had said.

"Off you go now young man. Your mother is getting worried about you. And remember tolerate Seth. It will not be for very long." With that, she turned and continued prodding the laundry with her stick.

Joshua got up and left. He had felt a sense of comfort and peace in her presence. He thought about her words as he went back through the hamlet. Maybe Seth was not so bad. After all, he had no experience in blacksmithing and he must be finding it very hard to be taught by someone as young as Joshua.

"I will work very hard and lead him by my example," he thought. Joshua knew that within a few days, he himself would be able to forge horseshoes just as his father had done. He felt apprehensive, however, about dealing with customers. He knew he was a small boy and that older people would not treat him with respect. Seth, being much older, would be much better at the business end, talking about and receiving payments. By the time Joshua got to his house, it was beginning to get dark.

Chapter 6

A s he opened the door, his mother rushed towards him and threw her arms around him, tears streaming down her face.

"Joshua, where have you been? I've been so worried about you."

He just clung to her and sobbed. "I just miss my father so much."

I know, I know" she said, stroking his head.

They both cried and clung to each other for several minutes, and then Joshua gently pushed her away.

"Where is Seth?" he asked.

"Why? Didn't he find you? He went looking for you."

"Why Mama?"

"Because he and I were so worried. A Roman legionary came by and asked Seth if he could shoe two horses the day after tomorrow."

'What did he say?"

"He said he could. Then he went out looking for you."

Joshua blinked his mind racing. Only two days! Two days in which to learn how to swing the heavy hammer and forge the horseshoes. Then he would have to actually shoe two horses himself. He wanted to run out to the shed immediately and begin practicing. Instead, he sat down at the table and looked his mother in the eye.

"We need to talk Mama".

"What's wrong Joshua"?

"Well" he began slowly, "Seth is not able to swing the hammer and forge the horseshoes."

"Oh but he said that you were so much better than he at it. He said he will be happy to conduct the business, talk to the customers, discuss a price and handle the money."

Joshua felt rage building inside him again. He thought of Magdas' words. "Tolerate Seth for a few weeks." "But," he said quietly, "he knows nothing of our costs or charges."

"He seemed very able and competent, while he was talking to that Roman. I am sure those soldiers would not be too happy doing business with you or me."

Joshua nodded his head. His mother was right. They did need Seth for the business at the moment. He picked at the bread and cheese his mother had laid out on the table. He thought again of the task that lay ahead. Only two days to learn the blacksmith's trade. He jumped up from the table and went to the door.

"Mama I have to practice swinging the big hammer."

It was getting dark and hard to see in the shed. How he wished old Shep, his faithful sheepdog was still alive to keep him company.

Nevertheless, he picked up the heavy hammer and brought it down with a resounding bang onto the anvil. He was still feeling angry thinking about Seth, and swinging the hammer with all his strength, hitting the anvil in the same spot every time, brought him a great sense of pleasure and relief. He built up a steady tempo. His shoulder and arm ached, but he continued on and on until his legs began to tremble and his arm felt as though it was ready to fall off. A sense of pride came over him and, as he finally put the heavy hammer down, he knew he would be able to forge horseshoes.

If only he could practice with a horse to nail the shoes on. His father's words came back to him.

"Joshua, imagine you can do something. Get a clear picture of yourself doing it in your mind and you will be able to do it." He pictured his father stooping down beside the horse's tail, gently taking the horses hoof and holding it on his knees. With six nails held in his teeth and one in his hand, he would begin deftly nailing the shoe in place on the horses hoof.

Joshua had always felt scared by the huge animals when he was a little boy, but as he grew up, he had become more comfortable around them. Now however, the thought of holding the back leg of a horse and pounding nails into it seemed very scary to him. However, he knew it was something he would master just as his father had once done when he was learning the trade. He only hoped the soldiers would not realize that this was his first time.

It had become very dark in the shed as Joshua made his way to the door. Just as he neared the door, he tripped and fell. His knee hit something small and hard. He felt for it in the dark. It was a small round black pebble. He remembered the day his father had given him this pebble from the stream just after they had prayed together. Joshua had just told his father that he had felt God's presence very strongly. Ben-Gideon had handed his young son this round black pebble.

"There you are son. Every time you want to remember this moment and Gods presence, just roll this little pebble between your fingers."

Some days afterwards, Joshua had, to his dismay, lost the pebble. But now here it was again. Outside the sky shone with millions of stars. As he looked up Joshua was filled with a sense of wonder. He suddenly felt as though his father were standing beside him. He could almost feel the big man's hand on his shoulder. All of his doubts and fears dissolved. He just knew everything was going to be all right. For the first time since his father had died Joshua felt almost normal.

Chapter 7

As he came up to the door of the cottage, he heard his mother laughing. Once again, she was seated at the table with Seth, drinking wine. Seth looked up.

"Hi Josh."

"My name is Joshua," he snapped.

"Sorreeee." Seth said sarcastically. Then in a sulky voice, "I was just trying to be friendly. Hey kid, I got us some business with the Ros"

Joshua's father had always disapproved of the slang some people used when referring to the Romans.

"Just think," Seth continued, "the day after tomorrow we will make thirty shekels for shoeing two horses for the Ros."

"Thirty shekels" shouted Joshua, "That will hardly pay for the nails and the shoes."

"Hey, easy Josh. Sorry, Joshua. I didn't know what to charge and you went running off without telling us where you were going."

"I don't have to tell you anything," Joshua screamed.

There was a painful silence.

"Well, I guess you won't need my help. I know when I'm not welcome. Sorry for intruding." Seth got up to leave.

"Just a minute," said Dinah, Joshua's mother, a note of desperation in her voice . . . "Joshua did not mean to insult you. We really do need you Seth. Please don't leave us."

Seth glared at Joshua.

"Joshua," said Dinah, "You apologize to Seth right now."

Joshua saw the panic in his mother's eyes. He remembered her words "I am sure the Romans would not be too happy doing business with me a woman or you a boy." He realized with a terrible certainty that they really did need Seth. Joshua took a deep breath and his fingers searched for his pebble. As soon as his fingers curled around the little stone, he felt a great calmness and confidence. He looked Seth in the eye.

"I'm very sorry Seth." He said. "I did not mean to be rude. I guess I'm just worried that the Romans may think that we can always shoe their horses for fifteen shekels each. At those rates we would be losing a lot of money and would soon be out of business."

Seth sat back down. He thought about this problem.

"Well" he said after a moment, "I guess I'll just have to tell them I made a mistake and they'll have to pay more".

Joshua shook his head. He knew what tough negotiators the Romans were and how they haggled to get the lowest price, always accusing the Jews of trying to swindle and cheat them. He remembered his father bargaining long and hard to arrive at a price of seventy-five shekels for shoeing one horse. He had later told Joshua that although it was a low price, their family would probably benefit by getting a lot more business from the Roman garrison.

Joshua knew that the Romans would never agree to pay more than they had been quoted by Seth. But how could he get this across? Once again, he squeezed the little black pebble between his fingers and once again, his mind became instantly clear and calm.

"Seth," he said, "the Romans will never agree to us going back on our quote. They look down on us Jews and accuse us of cheating and trying to swindle them even when we give them a very fair price. But if we tell them that this was a special price, just this one time, just for the two you were talking to, and that in the future the price will be what we have always charged, seventy-five shekels for each horse, they may be happy."

"Whatever," yelled Seth? "Those damn Romans, they think we're their slaves. One day maybe the rebels will teach them a lesson they won't forget." Seth was referring to a band of rebellious Jews who had taken refuge in the mountains. They frequently came down and attacked the Romans. Joshua's father had told him that these men were wrong to murder and kill Romans.

Seth continued to yell and rant about the Romans and talk about the atrocities they had done to the Jews. It soon became apparent to

Joshua that Seth was working himself into a rage, maybe to give himself the courage to renegotiate the price of shoeing their horses. Of course, if he lost his temper with the Romans and was disrespectful, they would haul him off and flog him. That was a nice thought. However, being Romans they might also burn down the forge and take Joshua as well. The Romans dealt very harshly with any perceived disrespect towards them. As these thoughts went through his mind, Joshua became conscious of the pebble in his fingers. He felt a calm descend on him again and knew somehow that the price of shoeing the horses would work out all right.

He stood up and held out his hand to Seth.

"I would like to thank you and welcome you into our family business Seth." Instead of taking his hand, Seth reached over and punched Joshua playfully on the shoulder.

"You just practice shoeing horses," he said, "and I'll look after the business end of things, but we really will do need to buy a set of decent tools."

Once again, Joshua felt furious. He rolled the pebble around in his fingers and took a deep breath. As he exhaled, he pretended to yawn.

"I'm tired Seth. We have a big day tomorrow, I'm going to bed." He hoped Seth would get the point and leave. Instead, Seth poured himself more wine.

"That's good. You just take yourself off to bed. Your mama and I will just finish off this wine".

.Dinah just giggled nervously.

Joshua went over to the corner of the room and lay down on his bed of straw with his lovely goatskin blanket. He rolled his little pebble between his fingers, once more trying to calm his seething anger at this young upstart who was making himself right at home in their house. He tried hard not to listen to their whispered conversation, although he was conscious of his mother's giggles and laughter from time to time. In his mind, he went back to his visit earlier today with Magda.

Just thinking about the old woman and her intense eyes gave him a sense of wonder. He tried to remember her exact words:

"God loves you very dearly"; she had said, "so much so that He has a special task for you and only you. This special task will bring you great joy and blessings".

Joshua wondered what great task God had for him. Perhaps it was learning to shoe horses. Maybe he would become a renowned blacksmith and the Roman Emperor would send for him. He smiled at the thought, he Joshua Ben-Gideon, going to Rome to meet with the emperor. Just then, Seth whispered something that made his mother laugh out loud. Joshua felt angry with his mother. How could she entertain this young man? How could she laugh, and drink wine with him in their father's house? He thought about what Magda's words again.

"You will have to put up with Seth for a few weeks," she had told him. "Because it is God's will"

So this was something God was asking Joshua to do for Him.

He again rolled the pebble between his fingers. This time he felt a great calmness and a Presence. He felt a great peace come over him.

Then he heard Seth's voice.

"Well Dinah, I'd better be on my way. I'll see you tomorrow."

As he drifted off to sleep, Joshua heard the door close and his mother's whispered "Goodnight," but he was already dreaming.

He was in the blacksmithing shed. The Romans had brought the two horses for shoeing. He crouched down beside the first big animal and, with his back to the horses head; he reached down and gently took the horse's hoof up and into his lap. He then effortlessly set the new shoe onto the hoof and began nailing it into place. As each nail went home, he felt a thrill of pleasure at how easy the task was. It was as though he had been shoeing horses all his life. He also knew the horse felt peaceful and safe and enjoyed being shoed. When the shoeing was completed, he went outside into the warm morning sunshine. He looked up into the deep blue sky and whispered "Thank you God". As he said these words, a gentle breeze lifted him off his feet.

Suddenly he was on his father's shoulders. They were on their way to Bethlehem to buy supplies. Then there were two little angels flying along either side of him. He wondered if he could learn to fly just like them. As soon as he had this thought, he was flying. Just like a bird, he swooped up and down. He felt so free and full of life. Oh, it was so wonderful to be flying like a bird beside these two angels and soaring through the air. He decided to see how high up into the sky he could go. The angels followed him up, up, up. He leveled out and looked down and there beneath him was the sparkling little town of Bethlehem.

He was filled with such happiness and excitement that he thought he would burst. Then there were small fluffy clouds all around him. He decided to try to land on one of these clouds. It was like landing on a bag full of feathers. He landed down, enjoying the soft featherlike feeling and drifted off into a deep and happy slumber.

Chapter 8

Joshua awoke shortly after dawn. He thought about his dreams and felt a sense of excitement about the future. He got up quietly and crept out into the crisp morning air. His mother was still sleeping. He did not want to awaken her this early in the morning.

He lit the big fire in the forge and, as he did so, he thought about his father. Oh how he missed him. As soon as the fire was lit, he made his way slowly down to the stream at the end of the meadow.

As he splashed the cold water on his face, he rolled the pebble between his fingers and looked up at the large tree. He immediately felt a loving presence. He walked slowly towards the tree and fell to his knees. Tears streamed down his face. He suddenly felt filled with love, joy, and happiness. Everything was going to be all right. He just knew it. He tried to remember when he had last felt so much joy. Then he remembered. It was just like the days before Ben-Gideon took him on his two-day trips to Bethlehem.

Every six months Ben-Gideon went to Bethlehem to buy supplies. The days leading up to this event were so exciting that Joshua could hardly sleep. He went into the barn every day and fed Fuzz, their donkey. He would chatter away to Fuzz as he munched on his feed.

"Fuzz" he would say, "we are going to Bethlehem soon."

The donkey seemed to understand. It nodded its head. Oh how he had loved that dear little donkey. But Fuzz had gone missing a few days after their last trip to Bethlehem. Now as he dried himself off at the side of the stream he wondered how he would carry the blacksmithing supplies without his donkey.

Maybe Seth would be able to carry the heavy supplies. Thinking about Seth however, made him feel sad and angry, so he immediately put his mind back on God and his father and Bethlehem. Some of the happiest moments of his entire life had been making that trip every few months to the town of Bethlehem. Reflecting on these happy memories, he made his way back to the blacksmith's shed.

As soon as he entered, he went straight to the fire he had lit earlier and began fanning the embers with the big bellows. He was startled by a loud cough behind him. He turned around quickly and almost bumped into the big man standing behind him. The man looked very scary, and was holding a large scythe in his hand. It took a second for Joshua to realize that it was only Nathan, a neighbor, who frequently brought his scythe in to be sharpened.

"I heard that Seth is now running the business," he mumbled, gruffly as he handed Joshua the scythe and looked around. "So where is he?"

Joshua took the scythe saying, "Oh he will be here later on, but I can sharpen this while you wait if you like."

Nathan made a noise that sounded like "HUMPF" as he turned his back on Joshua and walked back to the door. He stood looking up at the sky. Joshua was a little scared of this man, as in fact were most of the people who lived in Rimmon. He was known as a man of few words and those few words were always shouted in a loud voice.

Joshua went to the back of the shed and began sharpening the scythe with his sharpening stone. As he honed the blade, he began to worry if Nathan would pay him or if he would decide to come back later and pay Seth. He tried to remember how his father handled customers like Nathan. Ben-Gideon would take the sharpened scythe from Joshua, stride over to Nathan, and say in a loud voice "that will be ten shekels Nathan."

He decided to try and act exactly like his father, although he had such butterflies in his stomach. Then he remembered his shiny black pebble. As his fingers curled around it, he immediately felt a great calm descend on him. In a few minutes, he had sharpened the scythe. He stood up holding the scythe and strode purposefully over to Nathan.

"That will be ten shekels, Nathan," he shouted loudly.

Nathan glared at him for a moment, and then, to Joshua's surprise he pulled out a pouch and handed Joshua ten coins. Then, without another word, he took his scythe, turned, and walked off.

Joshua was ecstatic. He had just earned money from his first customer and he had handled the whole deal with this most difficult man all by himself. He could not wait to tell his mama. Suddenly he realized that he was starving, as he had not had any food yet. He ran across to the house. As he opened the door, he heard his mother coughing. To his surprise, she was still lying in bed. She had not made any breakfast. He went over and knelt beside her.

"Mama" he whispered.

Her eyes fluttered open and she had a bad coughing fit.

"What time is it"? She asked in a raspy voice.

"It's morning time Mama Are you all right?"

He had never known his mother to miss making breakfast except for one or two days after his father had died. A look of panic came over her face as she struggled to sit up, but then, another fit of coughing overcame her. Joshua tried to get her to lie back down but she resisted. When she stopped coughing for a moment, she tried to talk in a raspy voice

"No. Joshua, I must get up. Please help me."

He helped her over to a stool by the table and she sat down with her head in her hands still coughing. When she could finally speak, she said. "Seth has eaten all our bread and honey and cheese and I have no money to buy more." A tear rolled down her cheek. Joshua grinned and triumphantly thrust his pocket full of coins onto the table.

"Look Mama, I just sharpened Nathan's scythe and he paid me. So now we can buy some bread and honey."

"You should have waited for me Joshua," a voice behind him said. Seth stepped around him and swept the coins up into his fist. "I handle the business end of things. Remember?"

"You weren't here when Nathan came to have his scythe sharpened," Joshua replied. "We have no bread in the house Seth, and Mama is very ill". He gave Seth his best imitation of his father's icy glare, which he had seen only on rare occasions.

Seth seemed to notice Joshua's mother for the first time. "What's wrong?" he asked.

She tried to answer but another fit of coughing overtook her.

"Oh my," Seth told her, "you look and sound like a dung heap. I think I'll go and get you some wine and my grandmothers herbal fever recipe."

"We need bread Seth" Joshua said crossly.

"Oh I don't think she'll be able to eat much with that cough. Probably choke yourself to death eating bread Dinah, eh?" At this, he roared with laughter.

Joshua had never wanted to hit someone as much in his whole life.

Seth must have seen the look on his face. He turned and started to leave.

"I'll come back later with Gramma's herbal tea. But I won't be sitting and drinking wine with you today Dinah. I don't want to catch whatever you've got. And you Joshua, you need to run back to the shed and start earning us some more money."

With that, Seth was gone before Joshua could pick up a stool and hurl it at him.

Dinah had a long coughing spasm and seemed to be having a hard time catching her breath. She let Joshua gently lead her back to bed. As soon as she was lying down, she closed her eyes and was sleeping almost immediately. Beads of sweat lined her forehead and her breathing sounded very raspy. Joshua got a rag and poured some cold water from the pitcher onto it. Gently he dabbed the cold cloth across his mother's forehead. He thought he saw a smile flit across her face for a second.

As he sat on the floor beside his mother, he turned these problems over in his mind. They had no money or food. He was starving. His mother would need some nourishment too if she were to get better. He rolled the little pebble around in his pocket and looked up to heaven.

"What is great about all this?"

He had no sooner said this out loud, than he remembered the big jar of money hidden in the shed under the big anvil. He kissed his mother on the cheek and ran to the shed. It took a lot of effort to slide the heavy anvil off the square of wood but he managed it eventually. He kept looking over his shoulder to make sure that no one came to the door or could see him. He said a silent prayer that Seth would not appear. He moved the wood and, putting his hand down, lifted the heavy jar of money out. He spilled a quantity of coins out onto the floor, and counted what he thought would be sufficient to keep them in food for two weeks.

He then put the rest back into the jar and placed it back in the hole. He covered it with the wood and dragged the anvil back over on top.

He then went back to the house and hid most of the money under the straw of his bed. His mother was still sleeping. He was in a little bit of a dilemma. His father had never left the blacksmith's forge unattended.

"You never know when a customer might come," he'd always said, "and if you aren't there to look after him, he might never come back."

However, Joshua had to buy some food for himself and his mother. As there was no one to look after the business, he would have to close the shed door for a while. He was very worried about his mother. He had never known her to look quite so ill. He wondered if he should go and talk to Magda about her, but he was so hungry that he felt weak. So he set off to buy some food.

His first stop was Jacob's farm where his mother had often bought eggs and honey or a chicken. On the way there, Joshua thought about what might help his mother to feel better. He seemed to remember hearing that chicken broth was good for many conditions. So, after he had bought some eggs and honey from Jacobs's wife, he turned back to her and asked, "Do you sell chicken broth or could you tell me how I would get some?" Jacob's wife asked him why he wanted chicken broth. He told her that his mother was very sick and that he had heard that broth was a good remedy.

Jacob's wife explained that the broth came from boiling a chicken in water. She told him that she had just started to cook a chicken and that if he came by a little later she would give him a jar of broth for his mother. He thanked her and went on his way to the next farm to buy some bread.

His next call was at Isaac's farm. Isaac and his wife ground wheat and sold flour. They also baked fresh honeyed rolls and lovely oven baked loaves. Although Joshua's mother usually made her own bread, she would occasionally buy some fresh bread from Isaacs as a special treat for her family. Isaac's place was a very long walk outside the village of Rimmon and by the time that Joshua got there, he was starving. He bought six honeyed rolls and two big loaves and put them in the bottom of the sack he carried.

When he had walked a little distance from the farm, back towards home, he sat down at the side of the path and, taking out a large loaf, began to munch on it. Oh, it tasted so delicious. Within a few minutes, he had devoured the whole loaf. It had tasted so good that he was tempted to take out the other loaf and eat it too. Then, he remembered his sick Mama, and stood up and made his way back towards Jacob's farm. As he came up to the house, Jacob's wife came to the door.

"Here you are Joshua, she said, "Give this to your mother and tell her I said I hope she feels better soon." She handed Joshua a jar of hot chicken broth. He thanked her and made his way back home.

Chapter 9

As he came up the path to his door, he heard his mother coughing and an icy fear gripped his heart. What if his mother died? He ran into the house. His mother was still lying on her bed of straw, just where he had left her. Her skin was very pale and her breathing, between spasms of coughing was very raspy. She seemed to be sicker than she had been when he had left her sleeping earlier in the day. She tried to sit up when she saw him but she was too weak and fell back down. Beside her was a bowl of foul smelling liquid.

"What is this?" Joshua asked, picking it up.

His mother started coughing again and in between coughs and gasping, she told him that Seth had brought it and told her to drink it. But, she said, just a few sips had made her feel sicker than before. Joshua took the bowl and set it well away from his mother. The smell of the rancid liquid made him feel nauseated and he was sure it was not helping his mother's condition. He wanted to hurl the bowl out into the meadow but he knew that doing so might upset his mother and would certainly infuriate Seth. Instead, he told his mother that he had bought some warm chicken broth and asked her if she would like to try some. She shook her head, as she was racked by another fit of coughing. She tried to smile and told him she would try some later. He shook his head, a worried frown on his forehead

"What can I do Mama?" He asked, feeling helpless.

She closed her eyes for a moment and then began coughing again. Between coughs, she managed to say "Get Magda".

Why hadn't he thought of that himself? He stood up.

"Will you be all right on your own while I'm away?" he asked.

"Of course she will". Seth suddenly came through the door . . . "Besides I am here to see to her" Seth turned to the sick woman. "I hope you drank all your herbal tea I brought you Dinah".

"She just finished it a few minutes ago Seth, but she seems to be worse now," Joshua lied as he kicked some straw over the bowl on the floor.

"Well Grandma used to always say if her tea didn't kill you it would cure you." He roared laughing as he delved into the sack of food on the table.

"What have we got here"? He asked. "What have you been hiding from me Joshua?" he asked. He pulled out the remaining loaf of bread. He set down a large jug of wine on the table, exclaiming. "Food at last! I thought you were never going to feed us," He tore a big hunk of the loaf and stuffed it into his mouth.

Joshua wanted to run at the big lout and punch him in the mouth but he caught his mother's eye as she gently shook her head before another bout of coughing overcame her. She looked so frightened and weak that Joshua knew he had to get her some help and fast. He started out the door just as Seth called out to him.

"That's right Joshua. You just go and see to the business while I have some supper and look after your mother". Seth obviously didn't know that he was going to fetch Magda.

Joshua ran all the way to Magda's house. He knocked on her door A few moments passed and she opened the door just as he was about to knock again.

"What's the matter Joshua?"

He breathlessly told her about his mother's terrible cough as she pulled her shawl on and followed him out of her house.

"Has she had anything to drink"? She asked as they walked.

He told her about Seth bringing some herbal tea but that she seemed to be worse after that. He told Magda that his mother had only taken a sip or two but that he had hidden the rest of it by their doorway under some straw. The old woman just shook her head as she walked beside Joshua. He felt so safe as he trotted along beside her. She was such a strong determined woman who seemed to know exactly what to do in scary situations like this one.

In no time at all they were back at Joshua's' house. His mother was still lying down and coughing all the time. Seth was seated at the table, which was now covered in breadcrumbs, and drinking wine from the jug. As soon as she entered the room, Magda bent down and brushing some straw away, picked up the bowl of Seth's herbal tea. She put her nose to it and smelled it. Then she dipped her finger into it and tasted it. Her face grimaced and she glared at Seth.

"What is this Seth?" When he did not answer, she said angrily "This wouldn't be Syrian bark by any chance."

"My grandmother always gave it to people who were sick" Seth replied.

"Yes and do you know how many people have died from drinking this poison?" With that, the old woman took the bowl and threw its contents out the front door.

She turned back to Seth. "Now I understand these good people have hired you to do a job, so I suggest you go out to the shed and start earning your keep young man." She fixed Seth with her steely eyes and he hopped up from the table and scurried out of the house. She then put her arm around Joshua.

"I will take care of your mama", she said. "I think you should go and see that that young man does some honest work."

"Will she be all right"? He asked, looking down at his mother.

"I hope so Joshua," the old woman said shaking her head, "I hope so".

Chapter 10

Joshua wandered over to the shed his heart heavy with fear. He had lost his father, was he also going to lose his mother as well? The thought was almost unthinkable but Magdas words "I hope so" kept ringing in his ears.

"Why'd you have to bring that old hag?" Seth whined as soon as Joshua walked into the shed. For a moment Joshua was not sure he understood what Seth was saying. When he realized that Seth was referring to Magda, he hesitated a moment while rolling his little black pebble between his fingers.

"Seth", he said in a calm voice, "why did you give my mother that poison brew and make her drink it"?

Seth looked down at his feet. Then he licked his lips and glanced around nervously. "I thought it would make her better. My Granma always gave it to our family".

"And is it true some of them died after drinking it?"

"Well y-yes, but she said they would have died anyway," Seth stammered.

Joshua shook his head. He felt very grown up suddenly. He fixed Seth with an icy glare.

"What have you done with the money you took yesterday?"

"I—I bought some wine for your mother and me, a—a—and I paid Granma for her brew"

Joshua paused before replying "Seth", he said, "Mama and I have hired you to help us in our business. You have already been paid some money and have eaten some meals. If you want to continue working for us then you will need to work and earn your pay."

Seth glared at him defiantly. Joshua glared back. Eventually Seth looked down.

"I won't swing that hammer to forge horseshoes," he said in a sulky voice.

"All right Seth. But I need you to sweep and clean out the shed."

Seth stared at him for a moment and then, to Joshua's amazement, stomped over to the broom and began sweeping out the shed.

Joshua rekindled the fire and when it was blazing began to practice forging horseshoes. He was astonished at how easy this task seemed now. He was swinging the hammer and forging horseshoes as though he had been doing it all his life. He was also amazed at how well Seth appeared to be cleaning out the big shed. He said a silent prayer of thanks and then realized that God was helping him in all that he was trying to achieve. He then began to pray that his mother would soon get better.

But soon he began to feel anxious and frightened again. What would he do if her illness became worse? What if she were to die? These thoughts filled him with dread. He felt an overwhelming urge to stop what he was doing and to rush back to the house and sit with her. He knew instinctively however that this was not the right thing to do at the moment. His mother would be relying on him to shoe horses and do the work his father had always done. So he redoubled his efforts, swinging the heavy hammer up and down. As he worked, a sense of peace descended on him. He knew that whatever lay ahead he would have the strength to deal with it.

"The cleaning is all done" Seth said behind him . . . "It's getting dark so I'm going home." There were beads of dirty sweat running down his face. The shed looked tidier and cleaner than it had in a long time. Joshua took a moment to look around the shed. Everything was in its place. He nodded to Seth.

"Thank you. The shed looks cleaner . . . I will need you here at dawn tomorrow to help light the fire. Seth."

"At dawn?" Seth said incredulously

"At dawn. The Romans always come in the early morning. They don't like to be kept waiting."

Seth turned his back and walked off.

Joshua smiled to himself. At last, he had stood up to Seth and finally got him to do some work. He doubted that Seth had worked up a sweat like that in a long time. Maybe he would work out all right as a helper after all.

He continued to swing the heavy hammer with ease until he realized how dark it was becoming. Then he dowsed the fire and made his way to his house all the while praying and rolling the little black bead between his fingers.

Magda came to the door as he entered. She led him outside, and pulled her shawl around her shoulders.

"Your mother is very ill," she said very solemnly.

Joshua looked into her eyes and he knew without words that his mother was dying . . . He began to cry softly. Magda hugged him . . . He could sense her heartfelt prayers on his behalf and he felt comforted. After a little while, he stopped crying. He looked into Magdas eyes and asked "How long?"

She returned his gaze with her intense blue eyes. She shook her head.

"I don't know Joshua But it will be in Gods' good time. I have to leave her now, as I have some wash to deliver, but I will return to be with her tomorrow. If you need me in the middle of the night, come and get me. Otherwise, I will return shortly after dawn. In the meantime, try to stay by her side as much as possible. Try and get her to drink some water." With that, Magda turned to leave.

"Please", he said, "wait just a minute." Joshua rushed into the house and came back out with the money he had hidden under his bed of straw. He thrust the coins into Magdas hand.

"I know you have had to leave some wash undone and may have missed some of your customers. I hope this will help,"

Magda looked at the coins and tears appeared in her eyes. "You are a very kind young man. There are not many in this village who have your kind heart." She closed her eyes and tilted her head upward. Once again, he felt her prayers of comfort. She then turned and strode away. He watched her go with a heavy heart. He really loved this wise old woman and felt a great sense of peace and comfort in her presence.

Then he turned and went into his house. His mother was still lying on her straw bed. Her breath was raspy and she tried to cough. She looked so white and frail. Joshua sat down beside her and began to stroke her hair. Her eyes fluttered open and she tried to smile. He looked into her eyes. Without speaking, he knew that she was dying.

Tears coursed down his cheeks. She reached out and took his hand. He felt her unspoken thought; "I am going to be with your father." The tears kept rolling down his cheeks. An uncontrollable sense of sadness and loss engulfed him. She squeezed his hand, and his other hand seemed to find that magical black pebble. He felt God's presence again. Almost immediately, he felt fatigued. He moved his body so that his back was against the wall. Then he very gently lifted his mother up into his arms and laid her across his lap. With his arms around her, he fell into a deep sleep.

Chapter 11

He awoke just as the first rays of dawn appeared in the cracks around the cottage door. Joshua looked down. His mother was still sleeping on his lap. Her colour was very white but her breathing did not seem quite as raspy as the night before. He looked down at her deathly white face and said a silent prayer for her. Immediately her eyes fluttered and she smiled at him and began coughing. He stroked her hair.

"Mama." He said, "I have to go and shoe two horses for the Romans". She tried to say something but was unable to speak, because of a fit of coughing.

"It's okay Mama. Magda is coming to take care of you and I will be back as soon as I can".

As his mother nodded and smiled at him, he took her head off his lap and laid her down. He looked into her beautiful eyes for several minutes. They both knew that God wanted her. He was hesitant to leave her but he knew he had an important job to do. Her eyes fluttered and she fell back asleep again and he knew it was time to go. He kissed her, then stood up and went out to the shed.

He lit the fire and, when it was going, he made his way down to the stream. He felt as if he were in a fog. His mind was slow and he could not seem to think clearly. After he had bathed, he tried to pray but soon gave up and made his way back to the shed, where he found two legionaries standing beside their horses waiting for him. They nodded, as he led the first horse in to be shod.

Almost without thinking, with his back to the horses head, he crouched down and tapped the horse's hind leg, just above the knee.

The horse raised his leg and, almost before he knew it, he had the horse's hoof held firmly on his lap. Deftly he pulled out the nails that held the old shoe in place, then back at the fire, began to forge the new horseshoe. He was aware that the soldiers were watching him as he worked.

As he dipped the new red-hot shoe in a basin of water, he noticed that Seth had arrived. Seth just stood with the soldiers nodding and grinning. Joshua took the horses hoof on his lap again and expertly nailed on the horseshoe. He was amazed at how easy this task was. It had seemed to be impossible just a few days ago.

In no time at all, he had both horses shod. He took the second horse by the reins and led it out to the front of the shed. One of the legionaries took out a purse and counted out thirty shekels to Seth. Seth started to explain in Hebrew that this was a one-time only offer and that the future price would be different, but the soldiers just gaped at him, obviously not comprehending what he was saying.

Joshua stepped forward. Speaking In Latin he explained that his father had died, and that Seth was his new business manager. He said that Seth had made an honest mistake in his price that in future the price would be much costly. The bigger of the two Romans looked at him and said "How much costly?"

When Joshua told him, he immediately handed over the extra money to Seth. Both legionaries then nodded respectfully to Joshua as they mounted their horses and rode off.

Joshua watched them ride off into the distance

"Hey. How'd you get the extra out of the Romans?" Seth asked.

Joshua just shook his head.

"Please watch the shed", he said, "I'm going to see how Mama is." He walked away leaving Seth shaking his head in puzzlement.

Chapter 12

As he left the shed, he saw Magda come out of the house. She called to him and he began to run. He knew instinctively that his worst fear was coming true. As he drew level with Magda she said "She is waiting for you". Magda took his hand and they both entered the cottage. His mother lay as he had left her, still looking ghostly white. She hardly seemed to be breathing at all. He dropped down beside her, took her in his arms and rocked her back and forth, back and forth. Her eyes fluttered open. She looked at him and whispered "God loves you Joshua".

She then closed her eyes. A funny rattle came out of her throat and Joshua felt her spirit leave her body. He continued to rock his mother's lifeless body back and forth. Soon, Magda shook him loose and he left the old woman alone with his mother's body.

He went outside into the bright sunshine. He had never felt so lonely or sad in his life. His father had died, and now his mother was gone. His favorite donkey, Fuzz, was gone as was his faithful beautiful dog, Shep. He was an orphan all alone in the world. Why? Why had God taken everyone he loved away? He sank down and cried and cried. He felt as though his insides had been ripped out of him. He felt oblivious to everything that was going on around him He became dimly aware of Seth shaking his shoulder.

"I'm sorry about your Mama," he said.

Sometime later Magda tried to talk to him. She knelt down beside him and began to chant a psalm to God. He felt Gods peace descend on him and soon fell into a deep sleep.

When he awoke a short time later, he suddenly remembered where he was and that his mother had died and he was all alone. He wondered if her body was still in their house.

Slowly and, with a feeling of dread, he rose to his feet and went inside. He found Seth asleep on the floor beside the table, an empty jug in his hand. On the other side of the table, laid out beneath a white sheet on her bed, lay the body of his mother. He took the sheet off her face. Her face looked so beautiful. Magda had brushed her hair and had dressed her in a clean, white, long gown . . . She looked so pretty and young. Tears streamed down his face as he lay down beside her and put his head next to hers.

He lay beside her remembering how they had baked bread together, how she had sat with him on her knee teaching him funny little rhymes and how she had always made him his favorite breakfast of bread and goats cheese. It was not long before he was fast asleep again.

He awoke to find a number of people around him. Magda was kneeling beside him and shaking his shoulder. The Rabbi Eliud was inside the room, as were Seth and a number of villagers. Magda very gently told him that he had to get up and that the time had come to bury his mother. He turned his head towards her body. She had been covered by the sheet again. He wanted to take the sheet away and to hold and rock her body in his arms one more time, to make believe she was still alive, to talk to her and hold her. However, he knew she was with God now, and that everything in the universe was exactly the way it was supposed to be, even though he wished it were otherwise.

He allowed himself to be led outside as the Rabbi Eliud intoned prayers inside the house. Then, with Magda at his side, he led the funeral procession with all the villagers around the back of the shed, where a grave had been dug, beside the little plot in which his father lay. He watched with great sadness, as his mother's body was lowered into the ground, and the villagers shoveled soil into the grave. Somehow, he was not quite sure how, he found his way back home and fell onto his bed of straw and wrapped his goatskin blanket around his body and wept.

Chapter 13

The weeks that followed his mother's death were the saddest and loneliest that Joshua had ever experienced. Every morning he awoke at dawn, and got up and went down to the creek to bathe. Although he tried to pray, he felt unable to do so. He seemed to know that God was beside him, but somehow he did not feel like talking to Him. Although he loved God, there did not seem much point in talking to Him.

On many mornings, there was a Roman legionary or a local villager wanting some work done when he got back from the creek. Although Seth was never there when the first customers arrived, he always appeared just as Joshua completed whatever job he was doing. He always sidled up to Joshua and asked, "How much are we charging?"

Joshua always told him, and then he strode over to the customer and said, "We have just finished your work," telling them what the charge was, and he always pocketed the money that they handed him.

At first, Joshua found this amusing. Here he was, doing all the work and Seth was swaggering around and talking to the customers as though he owned the place. He felt fairly sure that Seth would keep the money safe until it was needed.

Each day one or two neighbors would bring some food for Joshua as they expressed their condolences. He seldom felt very hungry and was quite happy to let Seth devour most of the food. Seth spent hours each day just sitting on the ground outside with his back to the shed, chewing on a blade of grass and gazing up at the clouds. Once or twice each day he would fetch two pails of water from the creek for Joshua.

This was the only job he did apart from taking the money customers paid.

When he was not busy working on a customer's job, Joshua spent much time tidying and organizing the tools in the shed. He did so in order to keep busy and because he had no wish to get into conversation with Seth.

In the late afternoon and just before dusk, Seth always disappeared. He returned about the time Joshua was closing up the shed, always carrying a jar of wine. He accompanied Joshua back into the empty house, and sat down at the table, sipping wine and staring into space. He had ceased asking Joshua if he would like some wine as Joshua had always refused, preferring to lie down in exhaustion on his bed. On most nights, Seth would end up sleeping on the floor beside the table in a drunken stupor, where Joshua always found him in the morning.

One night, a few hours before dawn, Joshua awoke to the sound of shouts and laughter that seemed to be coming from outside. He called out to Seth but got no reply. It was pitch black in the house, so he was very careful as he walked and felt ahead with his foot. He did not want to trip over Seth. To his surprise, Seth was not there. Joshua went outside.

It was a dark night with lots of clouds hiding the moon. There were chinks of light showing from the blacksmith's shed and the sound of guttural laughter. Joshua fearfully crept over and peeked through the partially opened door. Inside, sitting on the floor with two of his friends, was Seth. They had lit some candles and were passing a big carafe of wine to each other, laughing loudly as they each took a swig.

For an instant, Joshua felt furious. He wanted to stride in and tell them to get out of his shed, but he recognized Seth's companions, Adonai and Elam as two vagabonds. They were reputed to be often in drunken brawls and, on at least one occasion, had been arrested by the Romans for questioning. They were big, violent louts and Joshua knew he could be badly hurt if he confronted them. Sadly and silently, he made his way back to his bed where he lay down and wept, until eventually falling asleep.

The next morning after he had bathed in the stream and was lighting the fire in the shed he heard hoof beats approaching. Thinking it was a Roman legionary he went to the doorway. To his surprise, he saw Seth on a pony, trotting up the track to the shed. Seth dismounted grinning

"What do you think, Josh?" He had begun calling Joshua, Josh, again shortly after his mother had died and Joshua had neither the will nor the desire to correct him.

"I got him for a bargain. He'll be useful for when we need to get supplies and I can use him for getting around."

Joshua was at a loss for words. In all the years that his father had been a blacksmith, they had never been able to afford a pony. Their only purchase had been Fuzz the family donkey. His father had a strong opinion about horses and donkeys.

"Horses," he'd always say, "are for the elite like King Herod's soldiers and the Romans. Ordinary folk like us have donkeys."

Joshua knew that horses and ponies were very expensive compared to donkeys. He wondered where Seth had managed to find the money to buy an expensive pony. He just shook his head and went back to working on the fire, while Seth sat outside on a log stroking the pony's forehead.

After a while, he came into the shed. "I'm just going to take the pony and get some feed for him. I'll be back in a little while. Tell any customers that I'll be back soon to see to them". With that, he strode out, mounted the pony and trotted off.

Joshua continued to work on the fire. Suddenly a large whiff of smoke blew into his face and he staggered back and tripped over something, falling flat on his back. For a moment, the wind was knocked out of him. When he recovered and got to his feet he looked to see what it was that he had tripped over. It was the board under the anvil. With a shock, he realized that someone must have moved it. He dragged the anvil off the top and lifted the board up. He knelt down and putting his hand down the hole, lifted up the jar that held all his fathers' savings. The jar was completely empty. He sat back on his heels. All his family's wealth had been stolen. There was now no money to buy fresh supplies, none for food, or anything else that he might require. Was this where Seth had got the money to buy a pony?

Joshua did not feel rage or anger, just a deep sense of loss and betrayal that the young man, who, had been taken into the family business and given a livelihood, could do this to the Ben-Gideon family who had been so good to him. He knew that confronting Seth would be useless. He would just curse Joshua and deny any knowledge of it. In fact, Seth in a violent rage would probably beat him up and demand an apology. A terrible tiredness and sense of futility overcame the boy. Wearily he placed the empty jar back into the hole. He then pushed the board covering it, back into place and dragged the heavy anvil over the top. He sat down dejectedly beside the anvil. He just wanted to die. He wanted God to take him away to join his parents.

He felt for the little pebble and began rolling it between his fingers. As he did so he heard the sound of horse's hooves approaching. Thinking it might be Seth returning, he wiped his tearstained face on his sleeve and got up and marched purposefully to the door. He was not about to let Seth know he was upset or that he knew anything.

As he came outside, he saw two Roman legionaries approaching on horseback. As they got closer, he realized that it was the same two whose horses he had recently shod. They reined in, in front of the shed and nodded to Joshua. The younger of the two dismounted and pulled a small pouch from his belt. He handed it to Joshua.

"We heard about the recent death of your mother. I'm very sorry for your loss young man. I lost my own mother last year". A look of sadness came over the legionary's face as he said this. "You are an incredibly good blacksmith for someone so young. I took up a collection at the Garrison for you. All of the soldiers contributed. They all have mothers." He said sheepishly. He then turned and mounted his horse.

All Joshua could do was to nod his head. He was dumbstruck. To think that these Romans who were feared and despised by so many people could be so kind and gracious to him was unbelievable. Just before he rode off the young Roman turned back to Joshua.

"That fellow Seth who works for you, is he here?"

"Uh, no, he went on an errand."

"Well, he keeps some bad company and is well known to us. I wouldn't trust him too much if I were you. You might be better off looking for a different helper in your business." With that, he nodded to Joshua, reined his horse around and rode off behind his partner.

Joshua watched them canter back down the hill until they were out of sight. Then he went into the shed and emptied the pouch of coins onto the ground. He was amazed at the large amount of money. It was almost a month's work of shoeing horses every day. He said a quick prayer of thanks and began to look around for a good hiding place.

There would be no point in saving the money in his father's jar. Seth and his friends had already discovered that hiding place.

Within minutes, Joshua remembered that there was an old bird's nest up high on a beam where the ceiling met the wall. The bird had long since abandoned the nest after being disturbed by the smoke from the fire. Joshua climbed up and put the Roman purse into the nest. He had just climbed back down when he heard the sound of hooves approaching again. He arrived at the doorway just as Seth dismounted from the pony.

"I got him some carrots to eat. Ponies like carrots." Seth reached into his tunic and took out a carrot. He began feeding it to the pony. Joshua smiled and shook his head as he turned and went back to the fire. Although he still felt some anger towards Seth, he found it pleasant and amusing that Seth enjoyed feeding his pony.

As Joshua went about his daily tasks of cleaning the shed and rearranging his tools, he thought about the stolen money and wondered how he would be able to pay for new supplies for the business. They were running out of nails and strap iron and many other essential items. These supplies, he knew, would cost a lot more than the money he had just hidden. Even if he had enough money and could buy the needed supplies, what then? Seth would continue to take and spend everything he, Joshua, earned. If only his father were here. He would tell Joshua what to do. Then he remembered his father's words. "Always turn to God whenever you have a big problem Joshua."

Joshua had sudden urge to run down the meadow to the stream and talk with God.

He went outside and found Seth sleeping, sitting up, with his back against the wall. His pony was standing nearby grazing. Joshua gently shook Seth's shoulder. His eyes blinked open

"I have to go on an errand Seth," he said, "and I need you to take care of the business Seth."

"Oh, uh, sure How long will you be gone?"

"Not very long Seth. You could sweep the shed while I'm gone." Without saying another word Joshua strode off around his house and down the meadow to the stream

Chapter 14

The stream sparkled in the sunshine. Joshua stripped off his tunic and bathed. He then climbed out of the water and took his little black pebble into his hand. He walked down to the large tree, knelt down, closed his eyes, and firmly holding his pebble he whispered, "I need your help God." Almost immediately, a beautiful peacefulness came over him. He just knew he was in the wonderful presence of God his Almighty Father. He spent a long time just enjoying the peaceful presence of God.

"God," Joshua asked, "what should I do?"

"Come to Bethlehem". A voice in his head said.

A wonderful warm feeling enveloped him. He suddenly felt ecstatic with joy. Memories of his trips to Bethlehem with his father, Fuzz and Shep, flooded his mind. He sat down with his back to the tree, while he pondered what God had said to him. God had not said to go to Bethlehem to buy supplies. Nor, had He said to take Seth with him. No. He had said *"Come to Bethlehem"*. It was an invitation from God to him and him alone. As he pondered this, he realized that he was being asked to leave his home and business and the little town of Rimmon where he had grown up and spent his whole life. But none of this mattered. He was excited at the prospect of leaving Seth and going to Bethlehem.

Maybe he could get a job at the blacksmith's forge in Bethlehem where his father used to buy supplies. What was the man's name? It started with a Z. Zachariah. Yes, that was it. He wondered if the old man would remember him, and give him a job. Not that it really mattered.

If God wanted Joshua to go to Bethlehem then God would surely look after him.

He then spent some time planning. He knew it was important not to let Seth have any inkling of his plans. He also knew he would have to have enough food for the two-day journey. This meant that he would not be able to leave until he had bought the necessary food for the journey. His mother had always baked two huge loaves of bread and packed a big block of goat's cheese for them.

As they journeyed, every hour or two Joshua and his father would stop and munch on a tiny morsel of bread and cheese. His father had always made sure that Joshua had the bigger portion. After they had savored a mouthful of food, his father had always said, "Just a little bit further Joshua and we can have another feast." His father seemed to know every step of the journey and whenever Joshua had begun to feel thirsty, his father would immediately come upon a little brook or mountain stream where, together with Fuzz and Shep, they quenched their thirst. He wondered if he would be able to find his way alone to Bethlehem, but he immediately knew that somehow God would guide him there.

Looking up at the sun he realized it was getting late in the afternoon. Unfortunately, this meant he would have to wait until tomorrow before he could buy the food he would need for the journey. He was so excited at the prospect of going to Bethlehem that he wanted to leave as soon as possible.

He stood up and stretched. He felt strong, confident and excited as he made his way up the field towards the shed. When he was halfway up the meadow, he saw Seth's pony coming towards him down the hill. The animal looked so lonely and forlorn. Joshua realized that the poor animal was probably thirsty. He gently took the pony's mane and led him down the hill to the creek. The pony was very thirsty, drank a lot of water, and then looked at Joshua with grateful eyes. Joshua led him back to the shed. As he got to the shed, he met Nathan's wife, Eliza, coming out carrying food wrapped in a cloth. Unwrapping the cloth, she revealed two very large loaves of bread and a hunk of goat cheese.

"I brought you some bread I baked today, and some cheese Joshua," she said. "Seth is sleeping his head off at the back of the shed. He really is not a very good helper. I would find someone else if I were you." With that, she handed Joshua the food.

"Thank you so very much Eliza," he said, "this is so kind of you"

She nodded and looking down, said, "I am so sorry about your mama, Joshua. You truly are a remarkable young man and a credit to your parents. May God be with you." With that, she turned and walked back down the path to Rimmon.

He watched her walk away and felt a little sad that he could not say goodbye to this nice lady who he had known all his life. He turned and carried the tray of food back to the house. He found a sack bag hanging near the fireplace and put the loaves and the cheese into it. He then took it over to the back corner and piled some straw on top of it, before going back out to the shed.

He woke up Seth who was fast asleep at the rear of the shed. He blinked and then leapt to his feet.

"I uh, swept the shed like you asked." Then he recovered and glared at Joshua. "Where were you? You've been gone most of the afternoon."

Joshua looked him squarely in the eye. "You were asleep Seth." Seth looked down at the floor.

"Well," he said, "I cleaned the shed out. I didn't see you earn any money today." He muttered. Joshua just shook his head and walked back to the fire, which was almost out.

After a few minutes, Seth mumbled something about being finished for the day and walked out of the shed. He climbed onto his pony and rode off. Joshua wondered if he would return tonight with his big jar of wine as he usually did. It did not really matter as Joshua was excited planning his escape. He and his father had always left for Bethlehem at the crack of dawn, and Seth was usually asleep in a stupor until mid morning. Joshua wondered if there would be a full moon tonight. If so, he would like to leave sometime before dawn, just in case Seth awoke early and decided to come looking for him on his pony.

He wandered around the big shed for the last time, looking at the anvil, the fire pit, and, all his father's tools. How he wished he could take it all with him, or at least hide the tools in some safe place. But then he remembered God's invitation to him. He knew he had to leave everything behind. He put his mind firmly on the journey ahead, and considered what he would need. He remembered that his father had always carried the big staff "in case we meet any robbers or wolves." Joshua took the staff from the back of the shed and placed it near the door. His father had also carried a large knife and a flint stone, so that they could make a fire. He looked around and finding both these items placed them in the corner of the shed, near the door.

He remembered that his father had always carried a few spare coins in a false heel in his sandal, "Just in the unlikely event that we were to lose all our money Joshua." Joshua could never figure out how they could possibly lose all their money as his father had always taken such care with everything. Now that he was older, he realized that his father was taking precautions against robbers. So he took off his sandal and with his knife and pried off the heel. Then he carved out a hollow space. Climbing up to the bird's nest, he retrieved the pouch of coins. He was able to place five coins in the hollow of the heel before nailing it back onto his sandal. Then he tied the pouch with the rest of the money to his belt and tucked it inside his tunic.

He decided that he would leave everything he was going to take with him just inside the door of the shed up against the wall and hidden behind some old dirty sackcloth's. This way, Seth would not see any of it and become suspicious. He ran over to the house and came back with the sack of bread and cheese. He also remembered to bring his beloved goatskin blanket. He put it in the sack with his bread and cheese and then tied the end of the sack around a small stick the way he had seen his father do. The stick, with all his food and blanket, could be easily carried on his shoulder. He stored everything behind the shed door and then after one more last look around the big shed, he made his way back to his house.

Inside his house, he sat down on the little stool and looked around. It was as though he was seeing everything for the first time. He looked at his bed, the fireplace, and the big pan that his mother had used to make bread. Then he noticed what looked like a tray covered with a cloth beside the back door. He went over, picked it up and brought it back to the table. Underneath the cloth were three delicious honey rolls, two figs and a bowl of goat's milk. He remembered that some neighbor, he could not recall whom, frequently brought some food and left it inside the door, most evenings. He realized that he was very hungry. He lowered his eyes and gave thanks to God for the food and for the kind and generous neighbor. Then, he hungrily devoured the food. It had been a long time since he had enjoyed a meal as much as this. When he had finished he hid the tray under some straw in a corner. He did not want Seth to see that he had eaten the food because that would make Seth very angry.

He lay down on his bed and put his hands behind his head. For the first time since his mother's death, he felt totally at peace. He started thinking about his journey to Bethlehem. He decided that he should leave an hour before dawn. This would give him a good start. He knew the general direction to start his journey. His father had often pointed out landmarks along the way. He only hoped that he could remember them. Just as he was pondering this problem, the door opened and Seth came in carrying a big jar of wine. Joshua closed his eyes pretending to be asleep.

Seth sat down at the table and banged the big jar of wine down, slopping some over the table. He looked around until his eyes fastened on Joshua.

You awake Joshua?" he mumbled.

Joshua lay very still, pretending to be asleep. Seth looked at him intently for a minute and then looked around the room.

"What, no food? Didn't anyone bring our supper tonight? Doesn't anybody in this village care that Dinah's dead?" He then took a big slurp of wine and putting his elbows on the table, put his head in his hands. Joshua knew from experience that Seth would spend the rest of the night like this, taking occasional sips of wine and gazing into space. Joshua also knew that Seth had cared for his mother in his own way and was missing her. He sat there, night after night, sipping wine and gazing into space until he fell into a drunken stupor onto the floor. The only exception had been on the night when his friends had met him in the shed and they had stolen all the Ben-Gideon family's wealth. Joshua hoped that Seth had not invited any friends tonight. Somehow, as soon as he entertained this thought, he knew it was not so. It did not seem very long before Seth had fallen off the stool and was snoring on the floor.

Joshua lay in his bed gazing up at the ceiling. He was suddenly filled with sadness at the realization that, after tonight, he would never see his home again. He had lived all his life in this little house. He remembered waking to the smell of his mother's fresh baked bread, lying in his bed, with the sunlight streaming in and the birds chirping.

He used to awaken, so excited at the prospect of helping his father in the great shed at the back of the house. Even at four years old, Joshua flew out of bed, charged into the kitchen and grabbed a hunk of his mother's fresh baked bread, taken a swig from the pitcher of goat's milk on the table and shouted "Hi Mama" as he ran out the door to help light the fire in the big shed for his father. All the memories of his childhood and growing up in Rimmon came back to him especially his trips to Bethlehem. He was so excited that he wanted to get up and leave, but knew that he must wait until nearly dawn when the early sunlight would light the way. It was very late in the night before sleep finally came to him.

Chapter 15

It was pitch still dark when Joshua awoke. He could hear the sound of Seth snoring where he had fallen on the floor. He was filled with excitement that the time had come to put his plan into action. He knew that it was nearly dawn. Ever so quietly, he got up and made his way to the door. He felt with his foot for Seth's sleeping body, and gently he stepped over it. He opened the door and stepped out into bright silvery moonlight. He went over to the shed and collected everything he needed for his journey. Then with his knife in his belt, the big staff in one hand, and stick with food, money and goatskin over his shoulder, he set out for Bethlehem.

He knew the general direction and the path that he and his father had always followed. As a little boy, he had always been scared by the darkness and the possible dangers, but he had always felt safe in the presence of his father. He was surprised at how confident he now felt on his own. He looked up at the sky and saw a very beautiful bright star ahead. It seemed to be shining from the very direction towards which he was traveling, and he knew that God was helping him to find his way. He was full of excitement and purpose, knowing that he was doing what God wanted and requested of him.

He marched speedily in the direction of the star. It was not long before dawn broke and as the miles passed under his speeding feet, the sun rose high in the sky. The hills and the valleys sparkled in the morning sun and Joshua felt so happy and good to be alive. Every so often, he would see a rock or a tree or a stream and memories of his trips with his father would flood back. It was almost as if they were both together on this journey and in a way, he knew they were.

Finally, Joshua began to wilt. He felt tired and hungry. He walked for a little while further until the path dipped down and turned beside a gurgling brook. He remembered that he and his father had frequently stopped here for "a little feast". He smiled and sank down beside the brook and took the stick off his shoulder. He untied the sack and took out his food. He began to devour the loaf, but then remembered his father's words. "Only eat a little morsel Joshua. We have to make this last the journey." Joshua smiled and slowed down. He took a little bite of cheese and let it linger in his mouth, the way his father had taught him. Then he took a tiny bite of bread. After a few minutes, surprisingly, he felt quiet full. He knelt down beside the brook and cupping his hands, drank from it. Then he lay back with his hands behind his head, as he and his father had done and looked at the bright fluffy clouds.

He awoke with a start. For a second or two he did not know where he was. He suddenly remembered. He jumped to his feet. He looked up at the sky. The sun was just beyond its highest point. He realized that he had not been asleep for very long. Nevertheless, he had some ground to make up, and with his heart ablaze with energy and excitement, he set off again. Once more, he recognized rocks and trees that he remembered from his previous trips. It seemed to him amazing that he was finding his way all alone to Bethlehem. It was then he realized that God was guiding him. He strode purposefully forward and the miles just seemed to fly by.

Before he knew it, the sun was beginning to sink and the shadows started lengthening. He knew it was nearly time to bed down for the night. In the past with his father, they had always camped at the same place at night-fall. It was at a large cliff face with a shallow cave. His father had always lit a fire at the front of the cave and they had slept there until morning. Joshua began to wonder where this cliff was. Then suddenly, as he rounded a bend, there it was right in front of him. The cliff looked exactly as it always had and there at the bottom was the cave. In front was a burnt patch of grass where he and his father had lit their last fire. He walked over to it and gently traced the edges with his sandal. He remembered gathering firewood, and his father lighting the fire. They had sat there together and eaten bread and cheese. Then they had sat and gazed at the flames, each one thinking his own thoughts. It felt so nice being beside his father under the stars. Joshua loved being up late and out under the stars, beside the blazing fire. As it got late, his eyes would begin to droop. "Joshua it's time for bed." His father said and. Joshua crawled into the little cave beside his dog, on his goatskin blanket. He would pull the blanket over the top of both of them, and with his father and Fuzz outside, beside the fire, he went to sleep

He wished now, that he could have Shep with him. Poor Shep. One morning just before Fuzz, their donkey had been stolen. Shep had gone off chasing after a rabbit. That was Shep's favorite occupation, chasing rabbits. This time however he had not returned. The next day after searching for hours, they had found his body, bloody and mauled, by what looked like a wolf or a mountain cat. Joshua had cried himself to sleep night after night for weeks. Finally, his father had helped him deal with it one morning in the stream.

"Joshua, he had said, "please ask God what is great about this."

Joshua stopped crying for a few minutes and earnestly asked God "What is great about this?" In a flash, he knew that God would send him another friend one day that would love and protect him even more than his faithful Shep.

He pondered this memory now, as he collected firewood and lit the fire outside the cave. He soon had a fine blaze going and gave silent thanks to God and to his father for teaching him how to light a fire. He sat in front of the fire, eating tiny portions of bread and cheese and thinking about his life. He remembered his fourteenth birthday and his Bar Mitzvah. His parents had given him his beautiful goatskin blanket. The neighbors had come and showered him with money, which had gone into the big savings jar.

This reminded Joshua of Seth, and he wondered how he was managing on his first day alone, trying to manage the forge. He smiled as he imagined Seth's frustration at trying to handle customers while trying to figure out where Joshua was. He thought about the pony that Seth had bought with the Ben-Gideon family's wealth. He said a silent prayer for the poor beast. He knew Seth had no ability to look after the animal properly.

He felt his head beginning to nod from exhaustion. He stood up, knowing it was time to bed down for the night. A shiver of fear ran through him as he looked at the dark entrance of the cave on the other side of the fire. He had never slept in there alone without his faithful Shep beside him, and his father outside. He felt for the pebble. Then he looked up at the star filled sky. Almost directly overhead, was the bright star that Joshua had seen early in the morning when he had commenced his journey. The star seemed to bathe Joshua in a heavenly light and he felt Gods presence. His fear vanished and he lay down, wrapping himself in his beloved blanket, feeling warm and safe and excited about seeing Bethlehem tomorrow.

Chapter 16

Joshua awoke as the first rays of dawn sparkled on his face. He was wide-awake, almost immediately. He sat up and looked out of the cave. He saw the dying embers of the fire he had lit the night before. The dew on the bushes was glistening in the sunshine and the birds were chirping a beautiful morning song. He felt a great sense of excitement, knowing that shortly after midday he would be in Bethlehem, that busy town with its big Inn, lots of little houses and streets, and big bazaar. He knew that the next water he would come to was a small river just outside the town.

He opened his sack and had a few tiny bites of bread and cheese. When he had finished eating, he put the rest back into his sack. He had almost a whole loaf and a chunk of cheese left. That would be more than enough for his lunch just before he reached Bethlehem He knelt and gave thanks to God. Then he stood up, stretched, put his food and goatskin back into the sack and set off briskly.

He was amazed at how easily he was finding his way back over all the familiar landmarks. It truly was a beautiful day. He was conscious of the birds singing, the wildflowers swaying in the morning breeze, the musical rustling of leaves and everywhere the glorious sunshine. The miles slid by under his brisk pace. He came to the brow of a hill and there in the distance in front of him he saw at the crest of the next hill, a large white boulder. He remembered his father saying to him "See that boulder Joshua. When we get to that rock, you will see Bethlehem below in the valley". A surge of excitement ran through him and he quickened his pace. At the rate he was traveling, he might even reach Bethlehem before lunchtime.

The track he was on, twisted and turned its way down the side of the hill. He knew when he reached the bottom of the hill that the track would lead up towards the big white boulder and that he would be able to see the town. His pace quickened.

Just as he rounded the last curve before the bottom of the hill, three big ruffians jumped out of the bushes onto the track in front of him All three had raggedy dirty tunic's. They carried sharp pointed sticks, and wore bright bandannas on their foreheads and a triangular piece of cloth, masking their noses and mouths. The one in the middle had long black curly hair, right down his back and hard, brown eyes. The one on his right had short brown hair and a scar that ran from his eyebrow to his chin. They were both big and broad shouldered, much bigger than Joshua. The third one Joshua could not see too well, as he was partly hidden by the other two. He appeared to have short black hair and was considerably smaller than the other two.

"Where do you think you are going?" Curly-hair asked with a snarl

Joshua immediately put both hands on the staff he was holding and held it out defensively in front of him.

"I'm going to Bethlehem," he said loudly, with as much courage as he could muster. Out of the corner of his eye, he sensed some movement behind him. A fourth person had come out of the bushes and had dropped down on all fours behind him. He turned his head to try and see what was happening behind him. Curly-hair and his companions lunged forward. Joshua hastily took a step backwards and fell over the fourth ruffian who was kneeling behind him. As he went down, the back of his head hit a rock and he saw stars. Just before he lost consciousness, he felt rough hands searching him and then he thought he heard a deep-throated snarl and a yelp. Then everything went black.

Chapter 17

Joshua's head was throbbing. Soon he became aware of a big tongue licking his face. For a moment he thought he was back home in his house, and that his old sheep dog Shep was waking him up. He opened his eyes. To his surprise, he was lying on the ground out in the open and a big brown and white dog with soft brown eyes was licking his face. His head hurt a lot. Gently he felt the back of his head with his hand. There was a big bump, but there did not appear to be any blood. He sat up, feeling a little dizzy. Wagging his tail, the dog stepped back and looked quizzically at Joshua with his big brown eyes. Joshua remembered what had happened to him and looked around fearfully. The dog barked and wagged his tail.

Joshua felt for his purse. The purse with his money had gone. In a panic, he looked around for his sack of food and his precious goatskin. He saw the stick, and the torn sac that was tied to it, lying just beyond his feet. Unsteadily he rose to his feet and walked over to it. When he picked it up, he saw that the sack was empty. His precious goatskin, the only beloved memento from his past was gone. He did not care about the money, or his food, but his precious goatskin? This was too much to bear.

He sank down on his knees, tears streaming down his face. "Oh no" he cried, "Please God, not my goatskin."

The dog barked and ran off into the bushes. Joshua wept, feeling desolate. How could God allow all this to happen to him? Especially after he had started his journey to Bethlehem at God's request. His father's words came back to him. "Ask God what is great about this Joshua." But although he tried and tried, he could not think of anything that was great. Then just as he was beginning to feel hopeless, he heard a bark. He looked up. Standing in front of him, wagging his big brown tail and looking at him with those soft brown eyes, was the dog. He had just dropped something. Joshua looked. It was a brown goatskin blanket. For a second Joshua couldn't understand what was happening. Then with a whoop of excitement, he picked up his blanket.

He felt such a wave of gratitude to God and to this beautiful animal. He stretched out his arms around the dogs' neck and hugged him.

"Thank you, thank you, thank you."

The dog's tail wagged furiously in response.

"You are my friend." Joshua said, "And I will always be your friend." He said solemnly. Then looking around he saw what appeared to be a large piece of torn tunic lying on the ground. He walked over and picked it up. It had a large wet bloodstain on it. Joshua checked his own tunic. Apart from a slight tear under one sleeve, it appeared to be intact. He looked at the dog.

"Did you do this?" he asked it, "Did you chase off the robbers?"

The big dog barked and wagged his tail.

"Oh", said Joshua, "You're so beautiful. I just wish I could give you some food, but the robbers got it all."

The dog barked at him, then turned around, and began to trot away into the bushes. Joshua's heart sank. Just before he disappeared, the dog turned and looked at him and gave two short barks.

"What?" Joshua asked, "You want me to come?"

The dog barked again. It was almost as if it had said "yes". Joshua followed the dog deep into the undergrowth. He had a hard time keeping the dog in sight and wondered where he was being led. Suddenly the dog stopped and again began barking at him. When Joshua finally caught up, there, at the dogs feet lay a large broken piece of blood-splattered loaf. Nearby, in the long grass, lay the hunk of cheese. Joshua looked around, just in case the robbers had also dropped the purse full of money but there was no sign of that. Not that it mattered too much. He still had a few coins in his sandal and amazingly, this dog had saved his precious blanket and most of the food. He broke off the end of the loaf and held it out to his new—found friend.

"Here," he said.

The dog gently took the bread from his hand and began to chew on it. Joshua then broke off the part with blood and dropped it on the ground, intending to discard it but the dog immediately leapt on it and swallowed it down. Joshua laughed.

"You don't mind a bit of robber blood my friend, do you?" He then sat down and gave thanks to God. Together he and the dog shared the last of his bread and cheese. As he ate, he marveled that God had sent him this wonderful dog to be his friend and protector. He looked at the dog.

"Will you be my friend forever?" he asked the dog.

The dog barked happily and wagged his tail.

"What is your name?" The big dog looked at him quizzically with his head on one side. Starting with Bart,. Joshua began naming off names of everyone he could think of. The dog just kept looking at him, his big brown eyes looking puzzled. After trying several names, Joshua suddenly remembered a little boy called Sasha who liked Joshua and often came into the shed holding his mother's hand.

"He just had to come and say hi to you Joshua," the little boy's mother said. Joshua always bent down and gave the little boy a present he had put away for him. Sometimes it was a piece of string, or a piece of metal that looked like a miniature man. One time he had made a little ball out of rags and string for little Sasha He loved to watch the delight on the little boy's face.

Now as he looked at this beautiful dog he said "How about Sasha?"

The dog nodded its head and gave a joyful bark. Joshua grinned.

"Sasha it is" and he grabbed his new friend and hugged and hugged him. He felt deliriously happy. At last he had a friend. He knew he would be safe from robbers or any other dangers with Sasha by his side.

After a long time he set off back to the trail, with Sasha, and started climbing the steep hill up to the big white boulder. It was not long until they reached the boulder and the top of the hill. There, below them, sparkling in the warm afternoon sunshine, was the little town of Bethlehem.

Joshua sat down on the grass, overcome at the beauty of the scene. Sasha sat down beside him. The boy put his arm around his friend and gazed with wonder at the little houses and the busy streets. The town looked truly huge to Joshua, compared to the little hamlet of Rimmon. He was full of pride and joy that he had made this journey all on his own. Then he looked at Sasha and realized that he might never have made it at all if it were not for this wonderful dog. He stroked him lovingly. Looking over Sasha's shoulder, he remembered that there was a little stream a few paces beyond a clump of bushes on his right.

"Come on Sasha," he said, "Let's go and bathe." Sasha seemed to understand perfectly. The dog stood up, barked, and started to run in front of Joshua through the bushes and down to the river. Joshua laughed and chased after him.

As they got to the river bank Joshua remembered the last time he and his father had bathed here. It had always been their last stop to refresh before they entered the town. Joshua started to take off his tunic, checking for his pouch, his fingers made contact with the little black pebble and he felt a surge of happiness that the robbers had not got it. He waded into the river, which was knee deep at this point. Sasha gave a happy bark and jumped off the bank after him, hitting the water with a big splash and drenching him. Joshua laughed and splashed water at his friend. Together they romped and played in the refreshing cool water until Joshua fell onto the riverbank, exhausted. Sasha sat down beside him panting. There they lay in the warm afternoon sunshine. As soon as the sun had warmed and dried them, Joshua put on his tunic and they set off for Bethlehem

Chapter 18

As they entered Bethlehem, Joshua gazed around. He never ceased to be amazed at the number of little children running around and the people all walking and talking. He made his way along the familiar street to the inn where he and his father had always stopped and had a meal. The inn was a large white building that stood out from the little houses because of its size. He paused at the front door, unsure whether he would be allowed to take Sasha in with him. He looked down into those soft brown eyes. He just could not bear the idea of leaving his beloved friend and protector outside while he went inside to eat.

"Come on Sasha" he said as he went into the Inn.

The dining room was full of people. There were four Roman legionaries sitting at one table and families at others. Joshua went to an empty table near the window that looked out onto the street. The last time that he and his father were here they had sat at the same table.

"Please sit," he said quietly to Sasha.

Sasha obediently sat down at his feet and then after a moment lay down with his head under the table. Joshua then remembered the money in his sandal. He took off his sandal under the table and pried off the heel with his knife, emptying the coins onto his hand. He then placed them in his pouch.

He felt a little worried and shy, as he had never ordered any food. His father had always done so. He tried to remember what his father had said. Joshua always had a treat, honey rolls, goat cheese and goat's milk. His father had wine and a loaf and cheese and tomatoes. They finished off with a basket of figs. He had just finished pondering this when a pretty girl with long black curly hair and lovely green eyes approached him. She seemed to be very young, not much older than Joshua himself.

"What would you like, sir"? she asked with a mischievous smile. Joshua was a little awestruck at being called sir, and being spoken to, by such an attractive girl. He forgot for a moment what he had planned to say. "I uh," he stammered.

"Oh what a lovely dog", the girl said glancing down and seeing Sasha lying under the table. "Is he yours?"

Joshua beamed with pride.

"His name is Sasha" he said smiling.

"What a lovely name. I might have a juicy bone for him somewhere in the kitchen." Sasha wagged his tail and they both laughed.

"Could I have some honey rolls, cheese and goats milk please" he asked looking into those pretty, green eyes.

She nodded shyly and smiled. Then shaking her head to one side and sending her black curly hair over one shoulder, she turned and walked towards the kitchen.

Joshua gazed out the window onto the sunlit street. It was so exciting being here on his own, in this bustling town. He felt so grown up. He wondered about the green-eyed girl. Did she live at the inn? He wondered what her name was. He was excited just thinking about her. He loved the way she had noticed Sasha and had promised to get him a bone. He was still thinking about her when she suddenly appeared with his food and a bone for Sasha. She put the tray of food on the table and, taking the bone off the tray, she bent down and handed the bone to Sasha. Sasha gently took the bone from her outstretched hand and wagged his tail.

"You're welcome, Sasha" she said standing up and smiling. She turned those enchanting green eyes on Joshua. "Are you staying in Bethlehem or just passing through?" This time Joshua met her gaze with confidence.

"Actually I am hoping to find work here," he said.

She frowned and thought for a moment.

"Jahleel is the innkeeper and also my father. He was just saying the other day that he wanted to hire someone to clean out the stable. But it is a very dirty job." she said, wrinkling her nose.

Joshua beamed with pleasure. "I would be delighted to do that for him, but do you know of anywhere that Sasha and I could spend the night."

He was not thinking about the Inn as he knew that he could not afford a room.

"Oh, we have no room at all here. The Roman legionaries have taken up our spare rooms." She said apologetically, "But I will ask my father if he knows of anywhere you can sleep. There might be room in the servants shack" but she shook her head as she said this indicating that she did not think so. She looked sad and troubled that she might not be able to help him. He smiled his charming little smile.

"Don't worry about it. Do you mind me asking, what is your name?"

"Anna," she replied, blushing.

"Anna, I would be very pleased to clean out your father's stable. Can you please ask him if he would like me to start straight away? And don't worry, Sasha and I will find somewhere to stay."

She nodded, still blushing, and turned and ran towards the kitchen.

He looked at the feast in front of him. Honey rolls were one of his favorite dishes. He realized how very hungry he was as he began eating this delicious meal. The cheese tasted so good, as did the goat's milk He daydreamed about Anna as he ate his meal. He was just finishing when Anna returned, smiling. She placed a bowl of figs in front of him.

"My father said you can begin as soon as you have finished your meal. He would also like you to help him fetch some water for the Inn later today".

Joshua picked up a delicious fig.

"Thank you Anna, how much for the meal?"

"Father said there will be no charge for the meal. He said he will count it towards your work for him."

He nodded at her, smiling. Anna turned to walk away but suddenly turned back and bent down and whispered in his ear.

"Make sure you ask him how much he will pay you for your work". She glanced quickly over her shoulder, and whispered "He sometimes likes people to work for nothing." Without another word she turned and hurried away. Joshua ate the rest of the figs in the bowl. When he was finished he felt a little unsure what to do. He was thinking about going into the kitchen to look for Anna or her father, when Anna came out of the kitchen and beckoned him. He got up and followed her, trailed by Sasha.

The kitchen was large and filled with the lovely aroma of cooking food. A big lady stood stirring a large pot of stew. Anna introduced her.

"This is my mamma, Sarah, and mama, this is Joshua"

She wiped her hand on her apron and nodded to Joshua.

"I am pleased to meet you Joshua, I hope you will be able to clean out the stable. It is a filthy mess. It's a wonder that poor Samson is still alive at all" Shaking her head she turned and went back to stirring the pot. Joshua followed Anna out of the kitchen to the back door of the Inn.

"Who is Samson?" he asked as he caught her up at the door.

"Oh. That's our ox who lives in the stable," she said over her shoulder.

They came out into a large courtyard at the rear of the Inn. Just beside the back door was a little platform with two water barrels on it. On their left, a few paces away, stood the little stable. There were flies buzzing around the doorway and a strong smell of dung coming from it. On the other side of the courtyard was a low long shed. Anna saw him glancing at it.

"That's where some of the hired help sleep", she said, "but I wouldn't recommend it."

"Why not?"

"Well for one thing, they are not very good company for someone like you" She blushed as she said this.

They came to the stable door and Joshua pushed it and went in. It took a moment for his eyes to adjust to the darkness after the bright sunshine. The smell was atrocious. The air was thick with flies, the floor was knee deep in dung and Samson the ox was over to one side lying down. He appeared to gaze mournfully at his visitors.

Joshua was appalled that the poor animal was living in such terrible conditions. It was as though, there had never been any fresh bedding laid down for Samson.

"Don't you have any fresh straw?" he asked Anna a little crossly.

"Over there" she said pointing towards the end of the shed across the yard. Looking out he saw there were piles of straw under a low lean-to at the end of the shed. She then left him for a moment and went around the side of the stable. She returned with a large shovel, which she handed to him. He could tell that she was embarrassed.

"Where do I put the dung?" he asked.

Without a word she led him out and around the back of the stable. They were in a beautiful green meadow, with long grass, that sloped down to a little stream. They walked along the top of the meadow and came to a very large pit. This large hole was filled with all sorts of rubbish.

"This is where we throw the dung," she said. On their way back to the stable she looked troubled. "I am so sorry Joshua that you have to do this terrible job." Joshua just smiled. He did not at all mind that it was a dirty job. He was used to doing dirty work. He was secretly pleased that he would be able to something to make poor Samson's life more comfortable. He looked down at Sasha, trailing along behind them. Sasha barked and wagged his tail. Anna and Joshua both bent down to pet him together and accidentally bumped heads as they did so. They both burst out laughing. For a moment they looked into each other's eyes. Then Anna stood up blushing.

"I, I have to go and help Mama", she said, as she scurried off.

Joshua watched her as she disappeared around the stable and then he got up and followed after her with Sasha. He wondered how he was going to tackle this huge job. At first he thought of shoveling all the dung out the door onto the courtyard. But the smell and the sight of such a big mound of dung, so close to the back door of the Inn, could cause a lot of concern. However, to move the dung, one shovelful at a time to the pit, would take him a lifetime. He looked around outside the stable. Leaning up against the side of the inn he saw a large flat cart with two long shafts. He realized that this was probably a cart used to get water. He ran over and taking the shafts in his hands, pulled the cart over to the stable door. With Samson between the shafts, he could haul the dung to the pit. He wondered if the Innkeeper would mind the water cart being used to haul dung.

He went into the stable and looked around. Over in one corner he spied what appeared to be a pile of rags. On closer inspection, he found it to be a large pile of old ripped and soiled clothing that someone had just dumped there. There was also an empty wooden pail. He carried two old ripped tunics out and tearing them down the middle, spread them out over the bottom of the cart. He then started moving dung, one shovelful at a time onto the cart. It was not too long before he had the cart piled high with dung. He was sweating and had to take his tunic off. He hung it up on a nail inside the stable. He looked around. He reckoned he had shoveled about a third of the dung.

"Come on Samson." he said to the ox. Sasha barked at the ox and wagged his tail. Slowly the ox clambered to his feet. Joshua helped him to back out of the stable and guided him between the shafts of the cart. He then fastened the harness to the cart and began to lead Samson to the pit.

At the pit it did not take long to unhitch the cart and allow it to tip the dung and the torn tunics into the rubbish dump. He was thrilled at how well he had done this task. He hugged Samson and rubbed the ox's forehead affectionately.

"Good work Samson" he said. Sasha barked as if to say "What about me?" Joshua laughed. "Yes Sasha, you helped too,"

He hitched Samson back to the cart and the three of them headed back to the stable. Once again, he laid down some old clothes in the cart to keep it clean and started shoveling dung onto it. He felt immensely happy and proud of his efforts. Somehow, it was as though he was doing exactly what God wanted him to do. It wasn't long before he had made a second and then a third trip to the pit and the stable was at last free of dung. He then took Samson and the cart down to the little stream. He unharnessed the ox and led him into the fresh sparkling water. Samson began drinking thirstily. Joshua took the empty pail he had brought and began pouring water over the ox. Then with the last of the old rags he began to rub him down, cleaning all the old manure off him. He looked at Samson and for a second he thought he saw the animal smile at him Sasha barked and frolicked around in the stream while all this was going on.

Joshua's last task before returning to the stable was to pour water on the cart and scrub it down. Although there was little sign of manure on the cart, it still had an odor. A few pails of water over the cart and a last pail over his own head and he was ready to go back to the stable.

As he harnessed Samson to the cart again, he could tell that the ox felt happy and clean. He led him up the meadow and across the courtyard to the long shed. There, at the lean-to he gathered a few armfuls of straw and placed them onto the cart. He led Samson back to the stable door and, taking armfuls of straw into the stable, he spread the straw all over the floor. The little stable already smelled better. He went out into the warm afternoon sunshine, pulling on his tunic. A big burly man with a beard was coming out the back door of the Inn. He looked as though he was rubbing sleep out of his eyes. He looked at Joshua.

"Are you the young man we've hired to clean out the stable?" he asked.

"Yes sir, I am Joshua Ben-Gideon", he said holding out his hand.

"I am the innkeeper, Jahleel" he said gruffly. "I see you have the water cart ready to fetch the water. When we have done that you can begin work on cleaning out the stable"

"Actually Jahleel, I have just finished cleaning out the stable." he said with a grin.

"What?"

The innkeeper looked flabbergasted. He strode over to the stable door and looked inside. He shook his head in astonishment.

"You did all this on your own?"

Joshua just nodded and grinned. Still shaking his head Jahleel brought Samson over to the stoop outside the back door and with Joshua's help slid the two almost empty water barrels onto the cart. Then he led the ox and cart round the side of the inn onto the dusty main street. Joshua strode along beside him and Sasha trailed along behind. The sun was very low in the sky. It would soon be dark. They walked in silence down the street.

"Anna tells me you have nowhere to stay tonight." Jahleel spoke very loudly, almost shouting. Joshua jumped startled.

"You could live in the stable now that it is clean and I will give you meals if you will be my helper?"

Joshua thought for moment. He remembered what Anna had told him, how her father liked people to work for him for little or no payment. He was quiet for a moment while he thought about what to say.

"That is kind of you sir, and I would definitely like to spend a night or two in your stable. But I am a blacksmith by trade. Tomorrow I intend to go to the Forge and ask Zachariah, the blacksmith, for a job. I am hopeful he will need some help as I really do need to earn some money."

Jahleel grunted. He glared straight ahead in silence. Joshua could tell he was not pleased. He was obviously a man quite used to having his own way with people he considered to be his servants.

They came to the well at the bottom of the hill. The well was right in the middle of the street. It had a little round wall around it. Joshua bent down and scooped a pail full of water up. He took it to the cart, emptying it into a water barrel. The Innkeeper sat on the back of the cart, watching him as he slowly filled the water barrel. When he had filled the first barrel, Joshua paused for moment, wiping the sweat from his brow. A little further down the street was the big shed that was the towns forge, where he and his father used to pick up supplies from Zachariah

Seeing Joshua looking wistfully at the forge, Jahleel scratched his head.

"I will tell you what Joshua. Consider the stable you have cleaned out as your home, for as long as you wish. I will give you meals and board you each week to be a helper, especially with fetching water."

He then got up and began to help Joshua, with another pail, to fill the second water barrel.

Joshua thought for a moment. He realized that Jahleel had still not offered him any money for his services.

"Thank you sir, I will help you each day with water, but I will still need to seek work at the forge. I am sure I will be able to manage both jobs."

Jahleel silently pondered what Joshua had said. He had a sad wistful look on his face. He had never encountered anyone who worked so hard and appeared to be as joyful as Joshua. He did not want to lose the services of this hard working, pleasant young man, but he was not in the habit of parting with money to his servants. He preferred instead to house them in the long shed and feed them with slops and leftovers. He believed them all to be lazy and dimwitted and they all lived up to this expectation. He had tried using them to fetch water in the past. They were so slow that this task generally took them all day long, so it was one of the few jobs that Jahleel had become used to doing himself.

It was getting dark as they arrived back at the inn. Together, they slid the heavy water barrels onto the stoop. Then the cart was unhitched and placed at the side of the Inn. Joshua led Samson back to the stable. Jahleel turned without a word and went into the Inn. Joshua was exhausted as well as hungry. He thought he would just lie down beside Samson, with Sasha, and rest for a few minutes, but within seconds, he was asleep.

Sasha barked loudly waking Joshua. Standing in the doorway was Anna, holding a candle in one hand and a tray of food in the other.

"It's all right Sasha, it's only me Anna" she said laughing, as she came into the stable. Under one arm she had a little three legged stool which she placed on the floor beside Joshua. Then she placed the tray of food on the stool and put the candle holder on the tray. The little flame from the candle gave the stable a warm glow.

"Oh Joshua, it looks so cozy and clean." She sat down beside him on the straw as he wiped the sleep from his eyes.

"But it still smells a little," she said wrinkling her nose. He sat up laughing.

"Anna, of course it smells. It is a stable."

She smiled shyly at him.

"You must be hungry." She said. "I brought you something to eat," she said pointing to the tray. Joshua's eyes sparkled when he saw the food on the tray. There was a big leg of roasted chicken, a loaf of bread, cheese, some small tomatoes, a bowl of figs and a small jug of wine. He started to eat ravenously.

As he ate, Anna told him about how pleased her father was with his work, and how amazed he was that Joshua had been able to clean out the whole stable in just one afternoon. She went on to talk about the Roman legionaries who had taken over much of the inn. Apparently two days ago, a Roman captain by the name of Remus, had come in and demanded some rooms for his soldiers who were in town to oversee the census. Jahleel had explained that all his rooms, except one, had been taken by visitors to the town. Captain Remus had then demanded to see the room, which was very small. The captain had then asked to see where Jahleel's family slept. It was a larger room at the rear of the Inn. He asked if there was a wine cellar in the inn. He then ordered the family to move their belongings to the wine cellar and said he would take the family's bedroom for himself. Two of his soldiers would take the small room and the rest of his soldiers would sleep in the dining room when the inn closed for the night. When Jahleel complained, the captain told him that he would be well paid for his services. The Inn had never had so much business and her father had to hire more help. Just as she was saying this, they heard a loud voice bellow "*ANNA*"

She got up quickly.

"That's my father. I have to get back and help,"

Without another word she hurried out into the night.

Joshua shared his meal with Sasha and in no time the tray was empty. He blew out the candle and lay down on the straw between Samson and Sasha. He felt so proud of his new home here in this warm little stable. And tomorrow he would go to the forge and see if he could find work. He put his arm around Sasha's neck and, pulling his goatskin blanket over them both, he lay there thinking about the wonderful exciting day he had just had.

Chapter 19

The sun was well up in the sky when Joshua awoke. Sunbeams were peeking through little cracks in the wall and one was shining directly on his face. He stirred and opened his eyes. Sasha immediately began licking his face. He laughed and sat up, rubbing his eyes. He inhaled deeply and smelt the smell of fresh hay and straw. There was also a trace of manure odor in the air. He wrinkled his nose a little and thought about Anna's words the previous night. She had not been too pleased about the smell. He wondered if his clothes might carry the smell and if this would offend her.

He thought for a moment about how he might solve this problem. Of course! He would hurry down to the stream and wash himself. He could even rinse out his tunic in the stream. Later in the day he would wash Samson down again. He gently stroked the big animal lying down beside him. He put his nose close to the animal and sure enough there was still a pretty strong smell of dung coming from Samson. This was to be expected. Poor Samson had been in a filthy state for such a longtime. He wondered if Anna could get him some soap from the Inn to scour Samson.

"Come on Sasha" he said as he made his way to the door. Sasha barked, jumped up and followed him outside. Together they made their way down the meadow to the stream in the warm morning sunshine. There was a feeling of magic in the air. Joshua waded into the stream and Sasha jumped in beside him and began frolicking around. Then Sasha barked. Joshua looked up. There on the opposite side of the stream the dog had spied a rabbit. The rabbit just crouched there, its ears sticking right up and its nose quivering. With another

71

bark, Sasha leapt towards the bank and the rabbit. The rabbit leapt forward and with two quick hops disappeared down a rabbit hole. Sasha charged up to the hole and began prancing around the spot where the little animal had disappeared, barking and wagging his tail. Joshua laughed.

"You missed him Sasha"

The dog looked at him, barked once more and then lay down with his head on his paws looking at the rabbit hole.

Joshua took off his tunic and rinsing it, wrung it out and placed it on the bank. Then he splashed the cold water over himself. The icy cold water was so refreshing. He bent his head in prayer and gave thanks. He felt so very grateful for his stable home, his best friend Sasha, the lovely Anna and his job at the Inn. He climbed out of the stream, put on his wet tunic and lay down in the warm sunshine beside his dog who was still gazing intently at the rabbit hole.

He decided that he would go to the forge and ask Zachariah for a job. He wondered if he would remember Joshua and his father. He thought about what he would say to Zachariah . . . He would offer to work for little or nothing until the blacksmith saw what a good and capable worker he was. Then maybe in a few weeks the old man might offer him a reasonable wage for his services. After all he did not need a lot of money. Jahleel had given him free lodgings in the stable and was providing his food. He felt sure he would be paid in the future. He had his best friend, Sasha and here he was living in this exciting town of Bethlehem. What more could a young man want?

He jumped to his feet.

"Come on Sasha".

The dog leapt up and with a last disappointed look at the rabbit hole, followed his master up the meadow. They walked around his little stable and across the courtyard. He went past the side of the Inn and onto the main street. There were not many people around, just a few little children playing in the street. It was still early in the morning and Joshua assumed a lot of people were still probably sleeping. He made his way past the town's well and nodded a cheerful "good morning" to a lady who was filling a pail with water. A few more paces and he came to the big shed that was the Forge.

The doors of the big shed were wide open. As he approached them Sasha started growling. Joshua looked at him in astonishment. Just before they entered, Sasha stopped dead and barked.

"What ?" Joshua asked, bewildered.

As he said this a young man appeared in the door way wearing a dirty torn tunic. He had short black hair and was smaller than Joshua. Sasha started growling.

"What do you want" the lad gruffly asked Joshua.

"I wish to talk with Zachariah."

Joshua tried to peer over the young man's shoulder into the dark interior of the forge. He thought he could make out three people huddled together near the back of the shed. He noticed that the big fire had not been lit.

"He's not here"

The youth glanced nervously at Sasha who was growling ferociously.

"I need to see him. When will he be here?"

"I don't know. He is sick and I am looking after the business for him. What do you want?"

Joshua thought he saw at least two of the figures coming slowly towards the door. Sasha began to growl and snarl and looked as though he was going to attack. Joshua grabbed his dog by the hair of his neck to restrain him. The youth took a frightened step backwards.

"Keep your dog away from me"

He continued to stumble backwards. Joshua turned away, pulling Sasha with him.

"Come on Sasha, let's go home" he said quietly walking away back up the main street.

"Do you think they were the ruffians who attacked me yesterday?"

Sasha barked and wagged his tail. He felt sure his dog was saying yes. But how could this be? Why would Zachariah let a bunch of ruffians look after his business? Joshua felt disappointed that he had not got a job at the forge. Perhaps when Zachariah got well again he would be pleased to have Joshua help him instead of those ruffians. As he rounded the Inn and walked towards the stable, Anna came out of the back door.

73

"Joshua, where have you been?" she asked a little crossly. "Mamma had made some fresh hot honey bread rolls for you. I'm sure they are cold by now."

"I'm sorry Anna. I was just out trying to get a job,"

"But why? You have a job here."

"I know but I need to earn some money Anna"

"Has my father not paid you yet"? She said, raising her eyebrows.

"Oh he said he will give me food and lodgings. I told him I need to earn a wage but that I will still help him with water every day."

They had entered the little stable. Anna was shaking her head, clearly upset with her father for not paying Joshua. She had placed a tray of food on his little stool. He sat down beside Samson and Anna sat down on the other side of the stool. He looked at the delicious tray of honeyed rolls, goat's milk and figs.

"You brought all this for me?"

"Yes but the rolls are probably cold"

He bowed his head in a silent prayer of thanks. Then he looked at Anna somewhat shyly.

"Are you hungry?"

She giggled nervously.

"I-I'm not supposed to eat with customers. But then you work here like me. So I suppose it would be all right."

She nervously broke off a portion of one of the rolls and began to nibble on it. It felt so nice and right to be sharing a meal with this pretty, young girl. He was glad that she had not mentioned the smell in the stable again.

She began to talk about the Romans and the amount of extra work she had to do.

"That reminds me," she said, "Papa would like you to paint the side wall of the Inn. Mama has made up a pail of whitewash for you."

Joshua said he would be delighted to do so.

"First, I have to wash down Samson. Could you get me some soap please Anna?"

She laughed delightedly, and pointed to the corner of the stable behind him. He had not noticed it before but she had placed a pitcher of water, a small wash bowl, a towel and some soap on the floor for him

"We do this for all our guests. And you are doing such marvelous work around here. But just don't tell Papa or I'll be in trouble."

Then she stood up and scurried out of the stable. Joshua felt a twinge of sadness. He suddenly missed her company. He thought about the way she giggled and the merriment in her eyes. Standing up he tossed the last honeyed roll to Sasha who had lain beside him watching every mouthful he had taken.

"Come on Sasha, we're going to wash Samson again"

Sasha barked and wagged his tail, as Joshua led Samson out of the stable.

Down at the stream he scrubbed Samson all over and then rinsed him down while Sasha lay down on the bank and watched the empty rabbit hole. There was a little bit of soap left so he scrubbed Samson down one more time and rinsed him with a pail of water.

"That should get rid of the smell Samson."

He led the ox back to the stable. Sasha got up and with one last disappointed look at the rabbit hole, barked and followed his master. Samson looked happy to be so clean. He even walked a little faster and seemed to hold his head up higher. He was led back into the stable and Joshua gave him a bundle of hay to eat.

Joshua went out into the courtyard and the warm sunshine. Sasha barked. One of the inn's servants was placing a rickety looking ladder against the back wall of the inn and a servant girl was placing a pail of whitewash on the ground beside it. They nodded to Joshua who smiled at them and said "Good morning." The young lady then went into the Inn and returned with a small brush. The servant man and woman were dressed very poorly in torn raggedy garments. They both looked dirty and unkempt. Joshua thanked them both, then dipped the brush in the whitewash and climbed the ladder and began painting the highest part of the wall. Sasha started barking loudly. Joshua could only paint a small area with the brush and had to climb down and dip his brush in the pail before climbing the ladder again. When he was on the ground, he told Sasha what he was doing.

"You will have to be quiet, or I might fall."

The dog seemed to understand because he lay down on the ground and became quiet, all the time watching his master on the ladder.

It was a very hot day and Joshua soon had to take his tunic off and lay it on a boulder that was at the corner of the Inn. Within an hour he had covered well over half the wall with whitewash. The part he had done sparkled in the sunshine. He had just about used up a whole pail of whitewash when the servant girl appeared with another one. He thanked her and began painting again. He no longer needed the ladder as he could now reach up to paint. He was however beginning to feel very tired and hungry and was just finishing when Jahleel suddenly appeared. He stood back and peered at the sparkling wall.

"Nice job Joshua, but you will have to leave that for a while. I need you to help me get water."

Joshua had just been considering taking a short break and having a rest. Instead he smiled cheerfully.

"All right"

They harnessed Samson and set off to the well with the water barrels. Jahleel started grumbling about the Roman Soldiers.

"I've never seen anyone use as much water as them. They are forever bathing. I've had to buy three more barrels. We will have to make two more trips today."

Joshua who was weary with fatigue and famished with hunger wondered if he would be able to do all this work without passing out. He rolled the little pebble around between his fingers. This triggered a deep calmness and he felt a fresh burst of energy.

They made two more trips to the well and it was beginning to get dark when they were finished. As he unhitched Samson and led him back to his stall, Joshua's legs trembled with fatigue. He was just about to lie down beside Samson and rest, when Anna appeared in the doorway. She had a tray of food and some wine. She placed it on the little stool.

"You didn't have any lunch, did you?" she said with mock anger.

He grinned and shook his head. He wanted to tell her he was too weary to eat, but knew she had made a lot of effort to bring him this meal. He began to eat the warm stew. It was delicious. As he ate he felt his energy returning. Anna lit a candle and the little stable was bathed in a warm light.

"The smell isn't so bad now. What did you do?"

"I just washed down Samson"

"Oh he looks so clean. But there is still a little bit of a smell here," she said wrinkling her nose. Then she pointed to the wall just above the straw.

"I bet that's it,"

She pointed at the brown manure stain all around the lower portion of the wall.

"I bet if you whitewashed that section of the wall, the smell would go away altogether.

Joshua nodded thoughtfully. Just then a loud bellow came from the rear door of the Inn.

"ANNA".

"Oh I have to go."

She jumped to her feet and ran out of the stable.

Joshua saved the last bit of stew for Sasha. When they had finished, he went out and retrieved the half pail of whitewash. It did not take him long to paint a small section of the wall all around the stable. He stood back and admired his work. The stable now looked a lot more comfortable than many of the small huts that poor people lived in. He took the empty pail to the back door of the Inn and was just returning to his stable when someone called his name. He looked around. The servants had lit a bonfire over beside the long shed on the other side of the courtyard. One of them was calling him. He went over. Two of the young men who worked at the inn were standing near the bonfire. The servant girl was slowly dancing around the flames and grinning at him. A couple of village youths were sitting on the grass drinking wine. The servant who had put the ladder out, earlier in the day, tried to give Joshua a carafe of wine he was holding.

"Here Joshua, have a drink."

He slurred his words. Joshua knew he was drunk. Memories of Seth came back to him and he suddenly felt scared. Sasha barked twice and Joshua knew he was saying "let's get out of here."

Joshua smiled politely.

"Thank you very much," he said. "But I still have some chores to do for the innkeeper . . . Maybe Sasha and I will join you some other time." With that he made his way back to his stable. He lay down beside Sasha and Samson and, pulling his goatskin blanket over him, gave a heartfelt prayer of thanks for his new home.

The next two days Joshua was busy from dawn until dusk, painting the inn, fetching water, helping to fix things and moving furniture. However, he was very happy in his new role as the inn's helper. Jahleel was almost friendly to him, as was his wife, Sarah, and of course Anna. Time flew by. He was so content in his cozy stable home where he slept like a log, in between Sasha and Samson, every night.

Chapter 20

The sun was beginning to set and a warm evening breeze blew a little dust up the main street. Joshua sat outside the inn with his back against the front wall. Sasha lay beside him, with his head in Joshua's lap. It had been another busy hardworking day. He had risen early and fixed the wheel on the water cart and then had made three trips to the town's well with. Jahleel. It was late afternoon when Joshua brushed Samson down, cleaned out the stable and put some fresh bedding for the weary animals. He had then helped Jahleel's wife by moving a table down to the basement cellar. She rewarded him with a large slice of bread and honey, some goat's milk and some wine.

Now as he sat in the afternoon sunshine on the main street outside the inn, he pondered on how lucky he was, and how good God was to him. As he contemplated his good fortune his eyes settled on a man leading a donkey, with a lady sitting astride the animal. As they got closer, and he saw the donkey more clearly, his mind went back to his father's donkey Fuzz. Oh, how he had loved that animal. He remembered when his father had first brought him out to see their new donkey. Joshua had run up, thrown his arms around the donkey, nuzzling his head into the animal's neck.

"He's so fuzzy!" he said.

Ben-Giddeon had laughed.

"Well, then this is what we'll call him, Joshua, Fuzz!"

Fuzz became another well-loved member of the family. Oh how he used to love riding on Fuzz's back when he was little, especially on those trips to Bethlehem for supplies. He remembered clearly the morning that Fuzz went missing from their home. After morning prayers with his father at the stream, he had gone into the barn to clean out Fuzz's stall. To his dismay, the stall was empty. He called out to his father, and they immediately searched the barn and went out into the meadows and surrounding country, calling Fuzz's name.

Joshua continued over the next weeks and months, everyday going into the woods and up the hill around his home, always asking neighbors and strangers alike if they had seen his donkey. No one had seen him. One night he overheard his father telling his mother that he was sure the donkey had been stolen. That night Joshua cried himself to sleep. A wave of sadness engulfed Joshua now, as he thought about the loss of Fuzz, his beloved father and mother and his home.

He became aware of Sasha's tail wagging and beating against the wall of the inn.

The man leading the donkey with the young woman was almost at the doorway. The man turned to the lady.

"You will soon be in a nice bed, just wait here."

He tethered the donkey to a post and went up the steps leading into the inn. Joshua looked at the donkey. It looked so very much like Fuzz, he thought. Then his eyes drifted to the lady sitting on the donkey. She smiled at him with the kindest, most gentle eyes he had ever seen. Without even thinking, he was on his feet moving towards her. He reached out and unconsciously began rubbing his hand up and down the donkey's forehead.

"Do you like him?" the lady asked.

Her voice was so gentle that, for an instant, Joshua was tongue-tied. Then suddenly he began babbling. He told the lady all about Fuzz and how he had been stolen. The donkey nodded as though he understood.

"I think he must know Fuzz!" she exclaimed, and they both laughed.

At that point, the man came out of the inn. He looked very dejected.

"Mary, they have no room. We will have to go to the next village."

His head sunk. Joshua looked at Mary's face. She looked very pale; he could tell she was sad and she looked exhausted.

"Oh Joseph," she sighed, "I am so tired and the baby is nearly here. Is there nowhere nearby where we can rest for the night?"

Her head also hung and Joshua spotted a glistening tear roll down her soft cheek. Suddenly, he felt compelled to grab Joseph's hand.

"Excuse me sir, I think I might be able to help you, please wait here for just one minute!"

Joshua ran into the inn to look for Jahleel Instead, the first person he saw was Sarah, Jahleel's wife.

"Would it be all right if I let that man and lady sleep in my stable for just a few nights?"

Sarah did not answer him right away. Joshua wondered if she were thinking about what her husband would say.

"The lady is having a baby, and I think it is going to be soon," he added.

At that, Sarah smiled.

"Of course Joshua, If that's what you want, but where, might I ask, will you sleep?"

"Oh, I will be fine. The weather is not too cold lately, and Sasha and I will find a nice place outside. It will only be for a few nights."

"Just as long as you don't get sick," Sarah said with a worried frown. "We need your help with all the visitors and soldiers here."

As if on cue a Roman legionary shouted in their direction,

"WOMAN. Can we have something to drink? We haven't got all day!"

At that, she scurried off.

As Joshua ran outside, he had a sudden thought, "What if my stable is unsuitable?" After all, he could tell that the visitors were not poor people. While he himself was proud of the home he had made, it was, nonetheless, a stable. Therefore, he hesitated as he breathlessly approached Mary and Joseph.

The man smiled at him.

"Well?" He asked.

"I have a place where you can rest and spend the night", Joshua told him, "but only if it's suitable for you. Please, follow me."

As he led them, he told Mary and Joseph that he was the innkeeper's helper and that the stable was his temporary home. He told them he had painted it himself. Shyly, he opened the stable door and led them in. For an instant, his heart swelled with pride. The whitewashed walls sparkled and his stall looked so tidy with the fresh straw bedding and goatskin with a little stool beside his bed. Samson the ox lifted his head to look at the visitors and seemed to smile. Sasha wagged his tail.

"Oh it's beautiful!" Mary said, "Did you paint this all yourself?"

Joshua nodded proudly.

"Mary, are you sure you should sleep in a stable tonight?" Joseph asked with concern. Mary laughed a soft and gentle laugh.

"Oh Joseph this is just right. It is just where I want to have the baby. Joshua has made it such a comfortable place. We will be warm, and I am so tired. Besides, we can eat in the inn, can't we?" She turned to Joshua. Joshua immediately nodded. She then asked him. "But where will you sleep?"

Joshua was so pleased that Mary had liked his home that he was lost for words again. He paused, then blurted," I will be fine; they will find me a place. I am the innkeeper's helper after all." He smiled proudly.

Mary turned and gently picked up the goatskin.

"What a lovely goatskin blanket. Is this yours?"

Joshua's eyes rested on Mary's soft hands caressing the skin.

"I would like you to have it. It will keep you warm and you might need it for the baby."

The lady smiled.

"You are very kind. Thank you."

Joseph fished a purse out.

"How much do they want for the stable tonight?"

"You don't have to pay anything, this is my stable."

Then he laughed.

"Well I guess I don't own it, but my working here helps pay for it."

He turned to Mary.

"I would like you to be my guests, for as long as you need to stay."

Joseph thrust some coins into Joshua's hands.

"Your kindness in giving up your home to us is greatly appreciated. Mary and I would like to thank you. This little bit of money will help you. I always like to pay people back when they are kind, so please take this money as our gift to you."

Joshua did not know what to say, so he just nodded.

"Thank you very much sir."

Joseph looked at Joshua and smiled gently.

"You can call me Joseph, and this is Mary."

Joshua felt a great sense of happiness. Joseph turned and patted him on the shoulder.

"Thank you so much Joshua, we will be very comfortable here for the night."

As Joshua turned to leave, he thought he should let them know about his ox.

"By the way, the ox is Samson. He's very friendly."

Samson's eyes darted up at the recognition of his name. He seemed to nod, as if he knew the statement just made was true. Joshua caught Mary's eye and they both laughed. Joseph looked confused and Mary quietly shared what she and Joshua already knew.

"The animals always nod when Joshua talks about them. They are his good friends."

With that, Joshua turned and bid the couple good night. Leaving them alone in their new, but temporary home, he wandered over to the back door of the inn and was just about to enter when Anna came out.

"There you are. Mama says you have given up your bed in the stable to a couple of strangers?"

The green flecks in her eyes sparkled as they darted from Joshua to the stable door.

"Oh yes," Joshua responded shyly. "Their names are Mary and Joseph, and Mary is going to have a baby, I think really soon!"

Anna turned a piece of worn soil with her toe.

"And just where, might I ask, are you going to sleep tonight?"

A slow smile warmed on Joshua's face.

"Oh don't worry Anna, Sasha and I will find a nice tree and sleep under the stars."

Anna looked concerned.

"What if you come across wolves or even snakes? You know very well they are out there!"

Joshua grimaced at the mention of snakes. He slowly gulped down the fear that began tickling his insides.

"Sasha will soon see them off, I'll be just fine," he replied bravely.

"Wait here," Anna called as she turned and went back inside. She soon returned with a large woven blanket. She threw it at Joshua, and he snatched it out of mid-air.

"This will help keep you warm."

Joshua held the blanket, and touched its woven threads.

"Is this your own blanket"?

"Just take it!"

Joshua folded the worn blanket, and started to thank Anna, but she had already disappeared inside the inn. Suddenly, Joshua noticed how dark it had become. He looked up at the sky. The first stars were beginning to twinkle, and it reminded him how each star seemed to be telling a story, as its light would dance through the darkened veil. Just as his mind began to play out what the stars were saying, there was a tap on his shoulder. He and Sasha both jumped in unison. Anna's shadowy figure stood before them.

"Have you eaten supper"?

With a sigh of relief, Joshua let her know that her mother had fed him earlier. The star light shone dimly into Anna's green eyes. Joshua liked the way her eyes crinkled at the sides when she was concerned about him. He longed to kiss her but did not feel brave enough to do so. He also had a lot on his mind. He had to go scout out a place for him and Sasha to sleep for the night, a place where there would be no wolves and no snakes!

"Sasha and I have to go find a place to sleep before it gets too dark."

"I wish I could come and help you find a good sleeping place, but Papa would be enraged at that. He insists I stay in the cellar after dark because of the soldiers. You know, if those soldiers didn't drink all night, you could sleep in the dining room," she frowned.

Joshua touched the edges of the blanket and smiled at her.

"Sasha and I will be just fine, now that you have given me this warm blanket, the night air won't touch me."

With that, he trotted off into the darkness with Sasha at his heels. His mind kept going back to Anna. She was so pretty and lovely. Sasha jumped up on his legs, as if telling him he needed to stop thinking about Anna, and find a place to sleep.

He walked quietly past the stable door. He could see a lamp flickering inside through the cracks in the stable wall. He would have loved to tap on the door and go sit at Mary's feet and talk to her. He felt so much respect for her and her husband Joseph.

On the other side of the courtyard at the back of the inn, some of the other servants had started their nightly fire and were beginning to sing and dance.

"Hey Joshua," one of the men shouted, "come on over and have a drink."

Joshua shook his head, waved and turned onto the path that led through the meadow. It seemed very dark in the meadow after the bright light from the bonfire, and he began to feel scared. Sasha's head nuzzled his leg and his cold nose licked his hand. Joshua looked up at the heavens. The sky was ablaze with stars and suddenly the night became magical . . . His fear suddenly evaporated and he felt a surge of happiness and excitement just as he used to feel the night before his birthday when his mom and dad told him that he was going to get a surprise in the morning.

His mind went back to Mary, Joseph, and his stable. He wondered if the baby was going to come tonight. He found himself standing under a large sycamore tree. He could see and hear the gurgling stream just below him. The moonbeams danced on the ripples in the water.

He looked back at the dark outline of the stable. A very bright star seemed to be shining directly over the stable, casting a beautiful heavenly glow onto the worn little building that was his home. It was as if God was thanking him for his work, and for giving up his new home to Mary and Joseph.

Joshua spread his blanket on the ground beside the tree, and lay his tired body on top of it, leaving enough room for Sasha. The dog licked his face and snuggled beside him, enjoying the comfort of the worn threads. As a cool breeze swept over them, Joshua pulled the end of the blanket to cover them both. He caught a fragrance of Anna in the blanket and wondered if she would be warm enough without it. That was his last thought as he drifted off to a deep sleep, his tired body relaxing after all his hard work. Sasha put his head on his master's chest, and sighed. The night air enveloped them both, and all was calm.

Chapter 21

At first, Joshua was not exactly sure what had awakened him. He sat bolt upright, before he realized what was happening. Sasha's ears were straight up, as he sniffed the night air. When they had gone to sleep, the air had seemed chilly, but now it felt as warm as the noonday sun. He threw the blanket off when he heard a voice. Sasha let out a deep-throated growl. Joshua knew that growl meant, "Someone is near!" Some people were coming from the other side of the stream, their voices sounding excited. He listened intently but could only hear snatches of their conversation.

"Why would God send an angel to us?"

Joshua could not hear the muffled reply. Words covered words until finally Joshua heard an older voice above the chatter.

"It must be the innkeeper's stable. See there is a bright star shining over it."

Joshua immediately became alarmed. The footsteps came closer and seemed to be heading towards him. He stood up and Sasha let out a sharp bark as if he were saying,

"This is not your home, its Joshua's."

He immediately stooped down and patted Sasha. He did not want the strangers to know he was there. He then spotted them coming to the other side of the stream. There were two older men and a young boy about eight years old. One of the men was carrying a baby lamb on his shoulder.

"Was that really an angel?" The young boy was asking.

"Well," one of the men replied, "it sure looked like an angel, and talked like an angel,"

"Did you see the bright light around her, and the way she suddenly appeared?"

The trio started across the stream.

"Oh, it's so cold," the young one said, visibly shivering.

Joshua instinctively stepped out from the tree, in front of them, as they started to climb up the bank.

"Hello," the young boy greeted him.

He reminded Joshua of himself a few short years ago, with his bright eager face and shock of curly black hair.

"Did you see the angel?" The young boy excitedly asked Joshua.

"No, what angel?"

The older man, who looked like the boy's father, replied in a deep voice that reminded Joshua of his own father.

"An angel of the Lord appeared to us as we were guarding our sheep and said she was bringing us glad tidings. He said to us

"Today in the town of David, a savior has been born to us. He is Christ the Lord."

He also said that we would find the baby in a stable wrapped in swaddling clothes. And suddenly there was a huge throng of angels, in the sky around, all singing and praising God."

Joshua immediately thought of Mary and Joseph and then he knew in his heart that the shepherd had received God's message. He suddenly understood God's plan. He felt so humbled that God had allowed him to prepare the stable for Mary and Joseph and God's Baby Son. He smiled at the shepherds.

"Come with me!" he exclaimed.

They followed him up the hill and round the side of the stable. The stable was bathed in heavenly light from the huge star that was shining right above it.

"Is the angel inside with the Baby King, Papa?" Asked the young boy.

"Hush now Daniel," The white bearded shepherd replied, "We must be very quiet, in case the little Baby is asleep."

They came to the door of the stable, which was wide open, with silver moon light streaming through. Joshua hesitated and then gently tapped his knuckles on the doorframe as he entered. Mary was seated on his little stool holding the Baby. Joseph was standing beside her and looking down at them. Mary looked over at Joshua and the three shepherds crowding in behind him. She smiled and gave a little nod to them all. He could almost hear her unspoken words, "Come in."

Slowly, reverently, they all walked inside and stopped a few paces away. Joshua was overcome with feelings of awe, love and peace and and happiness that he never imagined possible. Slowly he sank to his knees, as did his newfound friends. A heavenly energy infused the stable. Samson the big ox, his head turned, was looking at the Baby, seemingly smiling. On the other side of Mary and Joseph and the baby, the donkey was also lying down and gazing at the Baby with big, loving eyes. Joshua could feel the love that these two animals were feeling. Sasha was also lying down in front of him with his head on his paws gazing rapturously towards the baby.

The entire scene shimmered with God's love. Even the straw, the bedding that Joshua had put down on the floor yesterday seemed to sparkle. Although it was extremely calm and peaceful, there seemed to be music in the air, as if all the heavenly angels were singing. A warm breeze wafted through the doorway and he could smell the oranges from the orange grove across the street.

Mary gently laid the Baby in the manger, on top of Joshua's goat skinned blanket.

Joshua looked at Mary and Joseph, their eyes sparkling with tears of joy. He looked at his shepherd friends. Tears of joy were also spilling down their cheeks. He felt a strong affinity with the shepherds, the baby, Mary and Joseph, and the animals. Without a word being spoken, he could tell that every being within that stable was feeling the same feelings, thinking the same thoughts.

"Thank you Mary," he said in his heart. Without a single word to shatter the beautiful peace that enveloped the stable, Mary turned to Joshua.

"No Joshua, thank God." He heard her heart reply. David the shepherd boy, the two shepherds, and Joseph, all said "Thank you God," without a single word being spoken.

What a wonderful experience it was to know exactly what everyone was thinking and feeling without uttering a single word. It was as though everything inside the stable was in perfect harmony. It is impossible to say how long they were there, as everything was so still. The Baby's eyes suddenly opened and seemed to look directly into Joshua's soul.

He thought he would die with happiness. He wanted this feeling to never end.

At some point, night faded into dawn and suddenly the rays of the morning sun were streaming into the stable. Joshua felt and heard the oldest shepherd say, "We have to get back to our sheep."

The three shepherds silently rose from their knees, nodded to Mary and Joseph, and the eldest placed the baby lamb beside the manger. The three shepherds slowly backed out of the stable. Joshua felt conflicted. Part of him wanted to leave to talk to the shepherds and part of him wanted to stay in the stable. Mary smiled at him and once again read his thoughts.

"Go with your friends Joshua."

Reluctantly he rose to his feet and nodding to Mary and Joseph he backed out of the stable into the warm morning sunshine. The shepherds were waiting for him outside in the courtyard. As he caught up with them, they smiled, and together they all walked down into the meadow. When they reached the big tree, under which Joshua had fallen asleep the night before, they found Anna's large woven blanket still lying on the ground where he had left it. Joshua walked over and sat down on his blanket. Sasha followed him. He patted the blanket, signaling to his friends to be seated. They all sat down in a tight little circle. No one uttered a word. They all still felt the heavenly aura around them and were in awe at the beautiful scene they had left behind in the stable. It was as though they were under a magic spell that no one wanted to break. The morning sun sparkled off the dew on the grass. The water in the creek gurgled over pebbles and the birds chirped softly. Finally, the silence was broken by Daniel's eager voice.

"Can we go back to the stable every day and bring the Baby King a new born lamb Papa?"

His father looked lovingly at his son and put his arm around the boy's shoulders.

"Daniel," he said, "God has blessed us with a glimpse of heaven. None of us will ever forget the beautiful scene we have witnessed. However, God wants us to return to our families and our sheep. We must leave God's Holy Family alone now."

Joshua and the other shepherds nodded. It was as though God Himself had just spoken to them.

Daniel looked at Joshua.

"Will you come and visit us sometime?"

Joshua saw the sadness in the little boy's eyes. He reached over and gently laid his hand on Daniel's shoulder.

"Of course, I would love to Daniel"

"You will always be welcome in our home Joshua," Daniel's father said. "We live in the hills just to the right of the hillside over there," he said pointing to the large hill in the distance.

The shepherds then stood up, bowed their heads to him, and turned and walked away. Joshua sadly stroked Sasha's head as he watched them depart into the distance. In the short time he had spent with them, he already felt that they were the brothers he had always dreamed of having.

His father's words came back to him, "We are all part of God's family Joshua."

He watched the back's of the shepherds as they approached the top of the first small hill in the distance. Just as they were about to disappear over the hill Daniel turned and waved to Joshua. Joshua waved back and Sasha barked loudly and wagged his tail. Joshua patted his dog on the head.

"What would I do without you," he said as Sasha licked his face.

He looked up at the sun, which was just above the horizon. Every morning at this time when the sun was low in the sky, he cleaned out Samson's stall. In fact, it had only been a few days ago, he remembered, that he had cleaned and painted the stable for the first time. He remembered how filthy it had been and the long hours he had spent washing down Samson, painting the walls and putting in fresh bedding. It had taken him most of the week to get the stable looking nice and comfortable. Then he remembered Mary's words from last night,

"Oh, it's so beautiful!"

Once again, his heart swelled with pride. He began heading up the meadow towards the stable. The little building glowed in the early morning sunshine. He paused at the stable door, which was closed now, and he sensed with an inner certainty that the family was sound asleep. He also knew, although he was not sure how, that the animals were still clean in their bedding and the straw did not need changing. He was a little disappointed as he so much wanted to see them all again. He knew, however, that he would be needed later in the day. So with a heart filled with excitement, he went to the back door of the inn, carrying Anna's blanket.

He told Sasha to wait as he let himself in through the back door. A loud noise of snoring greeted him as he entered the big dining room. There were Romans sleeping everywhere. Some were asleep on chairs with their heads on tables. Others were sprawled on the floor and one was lying on his back, covering the whole length of one of the long tables. The air reeked of stale wine. Stepping quietly and carefully over bodies on the floor, he made his way into the kitchen and gently placed Anna's blanket on a table. Just then, the girl appeared in the doorway. Her face lit up with a smile when she saw him.

"Have you heard the news?"

He nodded, grinning and thinking she was referring to God's new Baby King.

"It's not something to really grin about," she scolded.

"What?" Joshua looked puzzled.

"Zacharia is gone", she said.

"I'm not sure what you are talking about, Anna."

"Then why did you just nod your head and grin?"

"Oh I thought you were going to tell me something else."

"What?"

"Never mind Anna, tell me about Zacharia"

"Zacharia, who owns the stable and blacksmithing business, has died".

Joshua shook his head in disbelief. His father's friend and supplier Zacharia was dead.

"How did it happen?" asked Joshua.

"Well, a couple of weeks ago he had a terrible accident. He was leading a horse out of the stable when it suddenly reared up, knocked him down and trampled all over him. It knocked him unconscious. Zacharia's boy, Aaron, and some of his friends are helping to run the business, but the day before yesterday her boy was arrested and taken away for questioning by the Romans. The next day Zacharia died. Now it looks like Ruth, Zacharia's widow will have to sell the business."

Joshua jumped down from the table he had been sitting on.

"Then I must go see if I can help her."

"What?" "How can you help?"

"I am a blacksmith you know," he said proudly, as he turned and went quickly back into the dining room, stepping over the soldier's bodies, as he made his way to the back door. Anna followed him. When they were outside again she said,

"But if you help Zacharia's widow you won't be able to work here. Who will keep Samson clean?" There were tears in her eyes.

"Don't worry Anna, I will still come here and help during the week."

Anna quickly bent forward and kissed him gently. Then she giggled and pushed him away and turned and ran back inside. He stood for a little while in the warm morning sunshine, and then set off around the inn to the main street.

Chapter 22

As he strode down the dusty main street, he was full of gratitude and awe Joshua reflected on all that had happened since yesterday; Mary and Joseph at home in his stable, the divinely beautiful Baby King lying on his goatskin, his newfound shepherd friends, his lovely Anna and the kiss that seemed to come from heaven and now the possibility of becoming a blacksmith like his father. Then he reflected on the death of Zacharia, the blacksmith they had purchased supplies from so often over the years. It was hard to believe that this old man was no longer at his forge. As he neared the end of the main street, he saw the big barn that was the town's stables and blacksmith's forge. Standing just outside the big barn doors was a frail looking little older woman who, he assumed, must be the widow Ruth. She held a walking stick in one hand and a sign in the other.

"Can I help you young man"?

She brushed a tear from her cheek.

"I'm sorry about your husband," Joshua said.

"Thank you, young man. And you are?"

"I am Joshua. Ben-Gideon. My father, used to buy all his supplies from your husband. My father had his own blacksmith forge in Rimmon. He taught me the trade."

"Do you want to buy the business?"

She held up the 'FOR SALE' sign she had been holding.

"That would be very nice but I'm afraid I have no money. Perhaps I could work for you and help you run the business?"

The widow thought for a moment and then said, "Come with me."

She led him across the street to her little house. They sat down on two stools facing each other across the kitchen table.

"I am in terrible trouble, Joshua. You see when my husband, Zacharia had his accident two weeks ago; I had to rely on our boy Aaron, to run the business with the help of his friends. Aaron is not really our son. He was Zacharia's sister's boy, but his mother died last year and we took him in. We tried to raise him and keep him out of trouble, but he made friends with some really bad boys. A couple of days ago the Romans arrested him. His so-called friends would often get drunk and go Roman baiting."

"What's Roman baiting?" asked Joshua.

The widow smiled and wiped a tear from her eye. She folded her arms and a far-away look came into her eyes.

"None of us here really like the Romans. They march around as if they own the place. They bring in their taxes and rules, telling us what to do!"

She glanced nervously over her shoulder.

"But they are our masters and they deal very harshly with anyone who opposes them. To give them their due they gave my husband a lot of business and they always paid their bills. In fact, my husband was doing very well shoeing their horses. Occasionally they would use our stables, like this last week when a lot of them came to town for the Census. Poor Zacharia, he had so much work to do . . . and . . . then . . ." her voice quivered, "and then he had his accident."

She paused and her eyes filled with tears, and her gaze drifted off into space.

"You were telling me about the boys Roman baiting," Joshua gently prompted.

"Oh, yes. Well the young men Aaron hung around with had little respect for the Romans. They liked to play all sorts of foolish pranks they called Roman baiting. I have heard they would hide behind walls or small hills with their slingshots, waiting for soldiers to ride by and then fire a stone at the flank of the last horse in the group. Or they would catch a viper snake, put it in a sack and leave it near a watering hole. Then they would wait for a soldier to come and either the horse would step on the snake and get bitten, or the soldier would open the sack to look and get bitten, himself. Oh, those silly boys had a whole host of foolish pranks. It wasn't enough for them to do these stupid things, but they would have to get drunk afterwards and brag about what they had done. Of course the Romans have their spies everywhere . . ." She let out a big sigh.

"So what happened after your husband's accident?"

"After Zachariah's accident, Aaron said he would do the chores but he could not forge horseshoes. He just never took an interest in the work when my husband tried to teach him. So anyway, at this time, there are ten horses in the stables that we are boarding for the soldiers who are staying up at the inn. They have to be fed and watered and have their straw changed every day. Aaron felt the work was too much for him, though, so he asked some of his friends to help. Those brats just helped themselves to all the money that my husband had saved and hidden in the barn. They did very little work looking after the horses, but they did get drunk a lot and now they've all got taken away by the Romans! And yesterday, we buried my husband."

A sob escaped her and she began to weep. She looked so old and frail that Joshua reached out and took her hand.

"What can I do to help?" he asked.

"Oh, I don't know," she sobbed, blowing her nose on a rag she pulled from her apron.

"The horses haven't been fed or watered in two days and two of them look very sick. I have done the best I can, but I have a bad leg and cannot carry a full pail of water. The soldiers will be very angry when they find their horses so neglected. Not only will they not pay me, but they may very well burn the forge down," she said, solemnly.

"Well we can't let that happen,"

Joshua said as he stood up and started to walk out the door.

"Where are you going?"

"To feed and water the horses and put down fresh straw."

"What, right now?"

"Of course!"

Without another word, he left the house, followed by Sasha. He crossed the street to the big barn. Inside it was as she had said. The horses did not look well at all. The stalls were filthy and swarming with flies. Two of the horses looked very thin and listless.

Joshua grabbed two pails and ran out to the well, which was just down the street. Filling the pails with water, he ran back to the stable. He set the first two pails before the two horses that appeared ill and they immediately began thirstily slurping the water. He found another two pails, ran back out to the well, and filled them. On his way back to the stable, he saw Zacharia's widow, standing in her doorway, leaning on her cane. She waved at him and he grinned at her as he raced back to the stables. She shook her head in wonderment, to think that such a young person would have so much energy and enthusiasm in tackling this mammoth task single handedly. As Joshua got to the doorway again, he saw a young boy, about ten years old, standing there looking at him.

"Hello," said Joshua as he ran past the boy.

He thought he heard the lad stammer a reply but was in too much of a hurry to stop. As he set down the two pails before the next two horses the boy came up to him.

"Could I have a job here please sir?"

It took a moment for Joshua to realize what the boy had said. He put his hands in his pocket and pulled out the five denari that Joseph had given to him. He held out the coins to the boy.

"You can have all this if you will help me feed, water, and put down fresh bedding for the horses." Joshua said, handing the boy the coins. The boy's eyes widened and lit up with excitement.

"Of course I will help you!"

"What's your name?"

"John," the boy answered shyly.

"Well John, first we have to fetch a pail of water for each of these horses. After that we will get feed for each of them and then we have to clean out their stalls and put fresh straw down."

Okay," said John, already snatching up the two empty pails.

"Just a minute Little John, I think two pails would be a little heavy for you to carry at once. How about you try one pail at a time?" he said, taking one of the pails from John's hand.

"Okay!"

John ran off with the single pail, eager to show Joshua what a good worker he could be. Joshua stooped down to pick up two empty pails. As he stood up, he felt lightheaded and suddenly thirsty and famished with hunger. He realized he had not eaten anything yet and that it was nearly midday. Wearily he trudged out of the big barn. Little John was already at the well filling his pail.

The blacksmith's widow was standing in her doorway and she called and beckoned to Joshua. As he got to the doorway, she turned and called over her shoulder.

"Come in."

He followed her into the kitchen. She had placed a big bowl of steaming stew on the table. There was also a loaf of bread and some goat's cheese and a platter with grapes and figs. In the middle of the table, there was a large goblet of wine.

"Sit down and eat," she motioned to one of the stools.

He sat down and began to eat ravenously. Within a few minutes, he had cleared the table of all the food. He leaned back in satisfaction

"Thank you so much. That was such a lovely meal."

"No Joshua, thank you so much. I think God sent you from Heaven," she smiled, "you must call me Ruth."

Joshua blushed at the praise.

"Secondly, about paying you,"

She emptied a purse full of coins onto the table in front of him.

"This is all I can pay you for your services for a few days. That is when the soldiers will come for their horses and will pay their bill. You say you can shoe horses?"

"Uh huh," he nodded.

"Well two of the horses will need shoes in a day or so. Can you do that?"

"Yes, But you don't have to pay me yet," he said eyeing the money on the table.

"Joshua I want to pay you. And I will," she said sternly fixing on him with her beady eyes. "Now here's what I will do. I will pay you fifty *denari* on Tuesday after the soldiers settle their accounts."

Joshua was astounded. His father hardly earned that much in a good month. He immediately shook his head.

"But—" he stammered.

"No buts, Joshua. You have saved my business and maybe even my life. These Romans can be very harsh to us Jews. Do you think those two sick horses will get better?"

Joshua pondered this for a minute.

"They may just be hungry and very thirsty. We will know better after I have fed them. By the way where is their feed kept?"

"It's in the large bin at the back of the barn, but there may not be enough feed for all the horses. Aaron was supposed to ride down to Ephron's farm and fetch two sacks of feed but he never did."

"I can do that, but not until tomorrow I'm afraid. I have to help Jahleel fetch water for the inn and clean out my stable there this afternoon. I will return here before dark and finish bedding the horses."

"Joshua," she said shaking her head, "you cannot possibly do all this work by yourself."

"I got used to hard work running my father's business after he died. Besides," he said looking out the door at Little John who was staggering towards the barn with a full pail of water, "I have a little helper."

He pointed to the boy.

"His name is John but I call him Little John."

"Oh that's Rachel's boy. Poor Rachel. Her husband disappeared six months ago. No one knows what happened to him. Rumor has it that the Roman's took him away for questioning. She struggles to raise her two boys by taking in people's laundry."

Joshua turned and looked at her.

"Ruth?"

"Yes?" she replied, raising her eyebrows.

"Would it be all right if I slept in the barn tonight? That way, I can get an early start in the morning."

"Of course you can Joshua. You could actually sleep here in my house, but that would set tongues wagging around here." She paused, and then said, "You mean to tell me that old Jahleel doesn't give you a room at the inn after all that you do?"

Joshua shook his head.

"The inn is full. The Roman soldiers have taken over most of the inn and Jahleel's family has had to move down to the cellars."

"Those Romans," she muttered mostly to herself as she turned and went back to the house.

Joshua looked up and saw that the sun was just overhead. It was midday. In a short while, Jahleel would be awake, and shouting for him to help get the water. Anna would be worrying about him. He longed to go back to his little stable and see Mary, Joseph and the Baby. He reckoned he had a little while left to feed and water the rest of the horses here, and if he had time, put down fresh straw bedding for them.

He began to feel very tired at the thought of all the work that lay ahead of him. If only he could go back to his own little stable and fall asleep beside the newborn Baby. Suddenly at the thought of the family in his stable, he no longer felt tired. He felt a surge of energy and excitement at the notion of finishing the chores here and getting back to the stable.

When he entered the barn, Little John was in the process of placing a full pail of water in front of the last horse.

"You have done this all on your own Little John?" Joshua's voice was full of amazement. Little John nodded proudly and they began to put feed in all the horses' feeding troughs. There was just enough for each horse. Joshua went out to the front of the barn and looked up at the sun. He saw that it was getting well into the afternoon. Jahleel would soon be up and looking for him. Just then, he saw a young woman approaching the barn with an infant in her arms. She had long dark hair and pretty, brown eyes. She was looking all around her and hardly seemed to notice Joshua.

"John!" she called loudly.

"I'm here Mama!"

Little John rushed out of the shed. Joshua grinned as the little boy flew into his mother's arms.

"Where were you?" She asked, hugging both of her children to her. "I was so worried."

"I've got a job now Mama."

He stuck his hand into his pocket, and pulled out the coins Joshua had given to him and thrust them into her hand.

"Five denari," she gasped, "where did you get all this?"

"From Joshua,"

Little John pointed to his boss matter-of-factly. She looked right at Joshua with her lovely brown eyes.

"You gave him all this money?"

Tongue-tied, Joshua could only nod.

"He . . . he has been earning it and he promised to help me again tomorrow."

Little John grinned and nodded his head exaggeratedly.

Joshua bent down so he was eye level with Little John.

"Thank you Little John, you were a great help to me today, and if your Mama lets you, would you like to help me again tomorrow?"

"Can I? Can I please Mama?"

She smiled.

"With all the money you have been given by this man today, you will need to work many days for it." Then she turned to Joshua and smiled shyly.

"I am Rachel."

Joshua's eyes met hers for a brief instant and then he quickly turned away, as his knees began to feel weak with the electricity that passed between them. Rachel interrupted his thoughts.

"I don't know quite how to thank you sir."

"Joshua," he stammered, "my name is Joshua."

"Well Joshua, you have paid my son more than I take in for three weeks work of doing laundry for my neighbors. John may help you each day for as long as you need him."

He suddenly felt very awkward. She sensed how he was feeling and smiled at him.

"Thank you again Joshua. Do you need John to stay now?"

Joshua shook his head,

"No, but thank you Rachel, I have to go to the inn now to help Jahleel. I will return here this evening to put fresh bedding down for the horses. Early tomorrow morning will be fine, for Little John to come."

"I will bring him here shortly after sunrise." Her eyes smiled warmly at him. "Good bye Joshua."

Little John began tugging her hand and telling her that he was starving.

Joshua quickly closed the big barn doors and ran back across the street to Ruth's house. He popped his head in through her open doorway and called out to Ruth that he was going to the inn and would return that evening. She did not answer. She was not in the house but he found her in the back garden picking figs from a small fig tree. He told her that he would be back before dark.

"I hope that. Jahleel is paying you handsomely, but I suspect that he isn't. You know Joshua, you would be quicker cutting through the meadow. You can see Jahleel's stable from here"

Sure enough, behind Ruth's house, the field sloped down to the little stream. On the other side of the little stream, up the hill, was his stable. His heart raced with joy when he saw it.

"There was a big bright star shining over that stable the other night" Ruth said. "It looked almost . . . ." Her eyes darted as she searched for the right word, "Heavenly."

Joshua smiled. He felt pleased and secretive about his knowledge of the family in the stable. He thanked Ruth and gave a loud whistle for Sasha, as he set off down the field.

When he came to the stream, he felt hot and dusty and realized he had not washed or prayed that day. The sun was still high in the sky and the day was very hot. He took off his tunic and bathed in the stream. Feeling refreshed and cooled, he gave thanks to God. He contemplated the three women in his life, Mary the Baby King's mother; he felt so much admiration and respect for her. Her quiet and gentle spirit filled his very being every time he was near her. He also felt, in a puzzling way, that she knew his every thought and that even now, as she sat in the stable with the baby, she knew and cared about what he was thinking.

His thoughts then turned to Anna. Yes, she was pretty, but then there was Rachel. Even though he had just met her, he had felt an overwhelming urge to touch her hand, to let her know that he felt something very special for her. Gazing into her brown eyes had made him feel something he had never felt before.

As Joshua rose from the stream, he looked to the heavens and asked God to bless these three special women. As he spoke these words, he also asked God to make sure and take special care of his mama, who at that moment he missed so very much.

He felt very weary as he trudged up the hill to his stable. His heart was, however, racing in anticipation. The door of the stable was open. Cautiously he looked around the door.

"Hello?" he called.

Mary was seated on his little stool between Samson the ox and their donkey. Beside her, the little Baby lay in the manger. His bright little eyes seemed to fix on Joshua.

"Come in Joshua," Mary smiled.

Joshua felt deliriously happy as he looked into the Baby's bright little eyes. Unconsciously he fell to his knees and rested his elbows on a fresh bale of hay that was like a small table. He wanted to tell Mary all about his new job as the village blacksmith, about the horses he had tended to, and about Rachel, Little John, and Anna. As his mind raced over all the information he wanted to share, Mary gently turned her head to him,

"Rest your weary head Joshua," she said, "You have worked so very hard today."

Once again, Joshua felt the presence of this special lady in his heart. It was as if she already knew all that had happened to him. Joshua put down his head on the bale of straw and immediately fell into a deep sleep. He began to dream. In his dream, four very beautiful angels with large wings came and lifted him up. Up, up, up he went in to the sky. They came to a large mountainside, covered in golden wheat. Ever so gently, they lowered him into the waving wheat. He felt as light as a feather. They began to roll him gently down along the mountainside. Somehow, his body seemed to float and stayed on top of the heads of the wheat. As he rolled, it was as though the heads of wheat were gently massaging all the sore muscles in his body. It felt so good. He rolled faster and faster. The feeling was wonderful. Finally, he came to the bottom of the mountain. The angels again gently took hold of him and carried him to a large pool that had steam rising from it. They lowered him in. It was steaming hot. At first it took his breath away, but as his body adjusted to the temperature it felt wonderful. All the tiredness and aches left his body. He began to feel lighter and lighter. It was a heavenly sensation. He looked up and saw the four angels sill hovering over the hot pool. His body began to float up above the pool and together with the angels, he began to rise higher into the sky.

He heard a man's voice whispering his name. He awoke with a start. Joseph was leaning over him, gently shaking his shoulder.

"Joshua,"

Joseph had such kind, gentle eyes. He reminded Joshua of his own father.

"When I was in the inn, they asked me if I knew where you were. I told them I would tell them if I saw you."

"How long have I been asleep?"

He felt as though he had just had the best sleep of his life. Mary smiled at him,

"Just a few minutes Joshua. You were so very tired."

Joshua felt a little embarrassed. He stood up and stretched.

"Well, I am afraid I have to borrow Samson, as we need to fetch water for the inn"

Joseph nodded,

"You can borrow our donkey too, if it will help. We call him Mica, and he is very good at carrying water pails with a rope across his back."

Joshua thought this would be marvelous. It could mean making a few less trips to the well. His eyes fell on the Baby. The Baby seemed to smile up at him with those two little bright eyes and he felt a surge of energy and love, enter his soul.

"Okay. Thanks and see you soon!"

He reached over and touched Samson to let him know it was time to go. Samson got to his feet and ever so slowly backed out of the stall into the hot sunshine. Then it was Mica's turn. The donkey nodded his head at the baby and, with a little coaxing from Joshua, backed into the yard alongside Samson. As Joshua was getting the cart harnessed to Samson,. Jahleel appeared. He was scratching his beard, and Joshua knew this meant he had something important to discuss. The innkeeper coughed and looked up at the sky, then down at his feet. He coughed once more before he spoke.

"Um, I hear you have a job as a blacksmith, working for the Zacharia's widow?"

Before Joshua could answer, he continued.

"Here is your pay for the last weeks work."

He thrust a pouch full of coins into Joshua's hand.

"I hope you will be able to stay and help me here."

Joshua's eyes widened in amazement. Since yesterday, he had received such a lot of money. He nodded to Jahleel.

"I will come every afternoon and help you, but I have to work at the forge every morning".

Jahleel nodded his head and looked relieved.

"Ok good. Now, let's go fetch the water."

Then he noticed Mica standing next to him and his eyes widened with surprise.

"Where did this donkey come from?" he asked Joshua.

"Oh, that's Mica. Mary and Joseph said that we can borrow him."

Joshua pointed towards the stable.

"Well that might just save us a trip or two," Jahleel remarked, "I have some small barrels that will fit on either side of his saddle."

He went into the inn, returned with the two small barrels, and secured them on Mica's back. Then he and Joshua heaved a large empty water barrel onto the cart. They set off down the dusty main street, with Samson pulling the cart and Joshua leading the donkey. Sasha trotted alongside.

Joshua felt so happy and full of energy. It was a beautiful day and he enjoyed every minute of the heavy work of filling the pails from the well and emptying them into the large barrel. It seemed no time at all before they returned to the inn and began their next trip to the well.

When they got back to the inn for the second time,. Jahleel was breathing heavily and was red in the face. He seemed to have a hard time keeping up with Joshua. After they had slid the second heavy barrel onto the porch outside the back door of the inn, the older man sat down on the porch beside the barrel.

"I think we need to rest for a few minutes." He gasped.

Joshua knew he still had to clean out his stable for Mary and Joseph and then finish cleaning out the blacksmith's stables and was anxious not to waste anytime resting.

"How about I go to the well and start? You have a rest and join me when you are ready."

Without waiting for a reply, he took Mica and Samson by their reins and led them in the direction of the well, leaving Jahleel sitting on the stoop sweating. The innkeeper breathed a big sigh of relief. He looked up to heaven.

"Thank you God. Thank you for that young man,"

He laid his head back against the water barrel and closed his eyes. Within seconds, he was snoring.

Joshua returned to the well and started filling the barrel. He was nearly finished when Little John came running towards him, his head hanging low.

"What's the matter Little John?"

Joshua bent down so he could look into the little boy's eyes.

"My mama is very sad,"

Little John looked down at his feet.

"Why? What happened?"

"We have to leave our house."

"Why?"

"I don't know. She told me to go outside and play. She is just crying and crying."

Joshua took the boys hand.

"Take me to your home".

He pulled Samson and Mica by their reins, and they started back towards the inn. About half way up the dusty main street, they stopped, outside a small house, not much bigger than a tiny shed. Little John pushed open the door and beckoned Joshua inside. After the bright sunlight, the room looked very dark and it took a while for Joshua's eyes to adjust. Then he saw the infant, Little John's baby brother lying on some blankets in the corner. A little further away Rachel was sitting on the floor crying softly. Joshua's heart went out to her. He reached out and touched her on the shoulder.

"What is it Rachel?"

She looked up at him with tear-filled eyes, then pushed herself to her feet and wiped her tears with her sleeves

"I'm sorry Joshua, I didn't hear you come in."

He took her hand

"What's happened Rachel?"

Her lip quivered as her lovely brown eyes looked into his. Tears started spilling onto her cheeks again.

"Barthomelew, the landlord who owns this house, he is putting us out next week."

A sob escaped her and his heart went out to her.

"But why?"

"Because I have not been able to pay the rent now for a number of weeks. He would have put us out tonight, but for the money John earned working for you."

She continued shaking and sobbing. Joshua's heart ached for her. He pulled her towards him and held her in his arms. She buried her face in his shoulder and sobbed. He felt so strong and protective just holding her. After a while, she looked up into his eyes and smiled.

"I'm sorry."

She looked embarrassed.

"How much does Nathanael want?"

"Twenty-five denari," she replied.

"That's all?"

Joshua smiled.

"That's an awful lot of money," she said firmly.

"No it's not," Joshua laughed. He opened up his pouch and spilled all his coins on the table. "There," he said, "That should pay him." Rachel's eyes opened wide.

"Oh, no, I can't possibly. Where did you get so much money Joshua?"

Joshua laughed.

"It keeps coming into my pouch like gold from heaven."

"I just can't accept this." She said, shaking her head firmly.

"Of course you can,"

His eyes danced with delight. He was so pleased that he was able to rescue this beautiful young woman and her children from losing their home.

"But I can never repay you,"

Tears began to well in Rachel's eyes again, and they slowly spilled onto her soft cheeks.

"Of course you can. Little John will be working for me, and if I pay him a little less each week, over a few weeks it will all be settled."

She gently rose on tiptoe and kissed him on the cheek.

"Thank you so very much Joshua".

Joshua blushed deeply.

"I uh . . . uh I . . . have to get back to the inn with this water for Jahleel."

He backed quickly out of the little house and took the animals by the reins. Sasha barked loudly and wagged his tail.

Rachel followed him out onto the street.

"When will you be finished at the inn?" she called.

"Soon I hope!"

With a wave of his hand he was off up the street leading Mica and Samson who was pulling the heavy cart. Sasha was running by his side, with his tail wagging.

"Thank you Joshua," Rachel yelled after him.

He turned to wave once more. Rachel and her son were still standing in the doorway of their home waving to him. Even from the inn, he could see the happy smiles on their faces. He felt so blessed that a few coins of his had saved them from disaster. He felt in his pouch. He still had some money left and he thought of the nice big meal he would order at the inn after he had cleaned out the stable. When he got back to the inn, Jahleel was pacing outside the back door.

"That took you long enough."

Joshua could tell that he was a little angry. He was not too worried however. He knew Jahleel's bark was worse than his bite. Together they slid the water barrel off the cart and then took the small barrels off Mica's back and into the inn.

Chapter 23

W hen the cart unhitched from Samson, Joshua led the two animals to the stable door. His heart was racing, as it always seemed to when he was in close proximity to the stable. He knocked softly on the open door.

"Come in Joshua,"

He heard Mary's call and stepped into the stable, leaving the animals outside.

"Aren't you going to bring in Samson and Mica?" Joseph asked.

"Oh ye—yes, but first I thought you might like me to clean out the stable and put some fresh bedding down for the animals."

Joseph put his hand on the boy's shoulders.

"Joshua you have worked hard enough today. I have already cleaned out the stable and put down fresh bedding."

Sure enough, the stable looked as clean and fresh as it would have if Joshua himself had cleaned it. Joshua felt both pleased and sad. He was pleased because he was beginning to feel very tired and hungry, but sad because he so wanted to do something nice for Mary and Joseph.

"I am just going over to the inn to fetch some food for a meal. I hope you can stay and eat with us?"

Joshua gazed with rapture at the little Baby.

"Thank you Joseph,"

He sat down on the straw close to the Baby. Mary was sitting on the little stool beside the Baby who was sleeping in the manger.

"Tell me about your parents Joshua"

Joshua started telling Mary all about his life as a little boy growing up in the village of Rimmon. He talked about his life as a blacksmith's son, how he used to help his father light the big fire every morning in the forge, how he and his father would go down to the stream and bathe and pray. He talked about their exciting journey every six months to Bethlehem, for supplies, and how much he had loved coming here with his father and Fuzz. As he was talking, Joseph entered the stable carrying a tray full of food. He set the tray down on the bale of hay that served as a table. There were three steaming bowls of stew and a loaf of bread. Joshua had not realized how hungry he was until he saw the steaming stew in front of him.

Joseph bowed his head and they all made a silent prayer of thanks to God. As they began eating, Joseph asked him about his other job.

"Anna tells me you may have a second job as the village blacksmith"?

Joshua then told them all about the widow Ruth, the Roman horses, and his helper Little John.

Joseph nodded and he told Joshua how much it had meant to him, helping his own father when he was young. That was how he had learned his trade. He looked lovingly at his baby son, asleep in the manager.

"One day, when he is old enough, he will help me and I will teach him to be a carpenter."

It was wonderful, Joshua thought, just sitting there and talking to Mary and Joseph. The Baby slept and there seemed to be stillness all around. Joshua could not ever recall feeling so happy.

When the meal was over Joseph gathered all the bowls and spoons. Joshua offered to take them back to the inn. Joseph however insisted that Joshua rest while he, Joseph, took them. Joshua was delighted to be able to stay and talk with Mary once more. As Joseph went out, a gust of wind caught the door and slammed it against the wall of the stable with a bang. The Baby awoke and started crying. Joshua immediately took his little pebble out of his pocket and gently rubbed it on the Baby's fingers. The Baby stopped crying at once and started to coo softly. Mary smiled.

"That was wonderful. What did you do?"

He told Mary all about his special black pebble that helped him to feel God's presence.

"Here, please take it. It will help calm the Baby if he gets upset,"

"But this was a special gift from your father", she said," I don't think I should take it."

"Please do," he urged her, "It will help your Baby and I would like you to have it."

He pressed the pebble into her hand. Mary smiled as she accepted the little black stone.

Joshua became aware of two bright little eyes watching him. He stopped talking, spellbound by those beautiful eyes. He thought his heart was going to burst with the love he felt for the little Infant. He moved over to the manger and sat on his heels gazing at the Baby. He saw the little hand, which was stretching out towards him. He wanted so much to touch it.

Yes," Mary said," you can touch him Joshua. Just give him your finger"

Joshua put his index finger out and the Baby wrapped his tiny hand around it. Joshua felt so much love and energy flowing into him that he almost stopped breathing. All his aches disappeared. Every doubt and fear he had ever entertained evaporated Just then, Joseph returned coughing loudly as he entered the stable. As the Baby let go of Joshua's hand, the boy knew that it was time for him to leave. He stood up.

"Well, I should be going now. Thank you for supper. I so very much enjoyed being here."

Mary and Joseph smiled.

"We loved having you with us" Mary said." I hope you will join us often for supper"

Joshua's eyes opened wide with delight.

"Really"?

"Really" said Joseph laughing.

"Thank you Joseph," he said as he backed out of the stable He nodded goodbye to Mary, who smiled back at him and glanced at the Baby, who seemed to have fallen asleep again. Then he was outside in the bright sunshine. The sky was brilliant blue, without a cloud, and a warm gentle breeze blew across the meadow.

He walked down the meadow with Sasha trotting beside him, his mind going over all the wonderful joyful emotions he had experienced in the stable. He looked at his finger that the Baby had held. It still felt warm and tingling. He put it to his lips and kissed it, remembering as he did so, the tiny little hand that had held it. Joshua's whole body felt lighter than air. Without knowing how he got there, he was suddenly outside the big barn. The sun had sunk very low in the sky and it was nearly dusk. He heard voices inside the barn. As he entered, he almost collided with Little John who was pushing a wheelbarrow full of manure.

"Hi Joshua, Mama is helping me and we have nearly finished cleaning and putting down fresh bedding".

Just inside the door, Rachel stood grinning. Her long curly, black hair tumbled down her back. Her brow had little drops of sweat and her face was streaked with dirt. She had a pitchfork in her hand.

"We have changed all the horses bedding," she said, "and washed down eight of them."

Her eyes twinkled with pride. Joshua was astonished. He had never seen a woman cleaning out a stable. He was also delighted. He had not been looking forward to the backbreaking task that Rachel and Little John had just completed.

"Where is your baby Rachel"?

"Oh I left him with Ruth. But Joshua, you know those two horses you were worried about? Well I think they are getting better."

She walked over to the two horses, which were standing up and looking curiously at Joshua. Both horses had been scrubbed down and looked a lot healthier than they had, earlier that day. As Joshua looked intently at them, the last rays of sunlight disappeared and it suddenly got very dark in the shed. Little John came in carrying a small oil lamp that Ruth had given to him.

"Ruth said you will need this," he said holding the lamp up high. "Show him the bed we made him Mama".

Little John led the way up to the end of the stable, carrying the lamp. Rachel took Joshua's hand, which he enjoyed immensely and led him to the last stall, which was empty. It had been cleaned and fresh straw bedding had been put down. In one corner, two blankets had been put down to make a bed. Beside the bed was a wooden box, on which Rachel had placed some bread and a cup of water.

"Mama thought you would be hungry Joshua"

Rachel blushed. Joshua knew she had probably given him the last food she had. He also knew that she very much wanted him to have it.

"Oh this is wonderful," he said dropping down and taking a bite of bread.

"Thank you so much Rachel."

The bread was very stale and hard as a rock. However, it was a gift straight from her heart.

"I am glad you like it Joshua. Come on," she said to her son, "We have to leave now so we can be back bright and early to help Joshua tomorrow. Goodnight." she said, as she led Little John out and into the dark night. Joshua's' mouth was still full of bread, so he had difficulty answering her.

Chapter 24

A s the first rays of sunshine came through the cracks of the wall, Joshua was suddenly wide-awake. He had been dreaming that the Baby was holding his finger. He woke feeling so alive and full of energy and excitement about this new day. He wanted to rush down through the creek and up the hill to his stable to see the Baby and Mary and Joseph. He entertained the thought of doing just that for a minute, but knew in his heart that it was not a good time to go visiting. He was sure the family was still asleep. Instead, he decided to walk down to the stream and have his morning wash and talk with God.

Within a couple of minutes, he was in the fresh creek. Sasha lay down on the bank and watched him as he washed his hands and face in the cold water. Looking up at the sky, he caught sight of the bright star shining above his stable. The star was beginning to fade as the morning sun became brighter but it still cast a heavenly glow over his stable. Joshua gave thanks for the family, especially the little Baby with the magic touch. Then he prayed for Rachel and her infant James and for Little John and the widow Ruth and the innkeeper,. Jahleel and his wife and Anna. Just then, Sasha barked.

"Oh yes God and Sasha too. Thank you for Sasha my best friend".

Sasha wagged his tail. Joshua thought he could sense his father right beside him in the creek. He was so happy that tears were rolling down his cheeks. He climbed out of the creek and dried his face and hands on his tunic before putting it on. Then he climbed the hill towards Ruth's house. He realized he was very hungry. He still had a few coins left. He decided that, when little John came to help him, he would send the boy to the inn to get some breakfast for them. He opened the big door of the barn and started the fire. He was just using the big bellows on the red-hot embers when Little John arrived. His eyes were red and he looked as though he had been crying. Joshua stopped what he was doing and looked at the little fellow.

"What's the matter Little John?"

John stood looking at the floor.

"Nothing," he said, "I've come to help."

Joshua studied the boy. He sensed the little boy had not eaten breakfast as he put his hand into his pouch and pulled out a few coins.

"How would you like to run down to the inn and buy us some bread and honey and goat's milk? We will eat breakfast when you get back."

Little John's eyes opened wide with surprise and delight.

"Really?" he asked.

"Really." said Joshua.

"All right."

He clamped his little fist around the coins and scampered off gleefully.

Joshua grinned and went back to his fire. Then he put some feed in all the horse troughs. It was the last of the feed and he wondered about buying some more. He checked the two horses that had been so ill the previous day. They were both doing fine and appeared to be normal and healthy. Sasha suddenly barked and wagged his tail. Joshua looked up. There standing in the doorway, holding a small sack, was Anna. At first he wondered if Little John had talked to her but then he realized they had probably passed each other and that Anna did not know he had sent Little John to the inn.

"Where did you go yesterday?" Anna asked. "I missed you."

Joshua felt guilty.

"Um . . . I had a lot of chores to do here. The Romans will be coming for their horses soon and I have so many things to do."

"But we need you at the inn."

He saw a tear in the corner of her eye.

"I know." he said softly. "But soon all these Roman soldiers will be gone and then I won't be so busy."

"I'm sure you will always be busy. You seem to love working and helping people," she said a little crossly.

"I am sorry,"

"Well," she said, "here's some breakfast for you," she handed him the food. "Now I have to run back and help Mama or I'll be in trouble. Will you come today?"

"Of course I will, later on, and thank you for the food Anna."

She threw her head back and walked off, leaving him standing there with the food in his hand. He felt bad for Anna. He knew she liked him a lot. She was very pretty but somehow since he had met Rachel, things looked different. Just then, he saw Rachel, across the street, handing her sleeping infant to Ruth. Anna had walked straight past her.

Rachel came across the street with some parchments in her hand. She looked so lovely with her black curly hair bobbing around her face, which was still streaked with some dirt from last night, but to Joshua she looked radiant. As she got closer, however he noticed her face was strained with fatigue and little worry lines. She put on her brave smile.

"Ruth asked me to give you this. She has written out the amount that the Romans owe when they come to ask you about their horses. The middle figure on the bill is just for stabling and feeding the horses. The big figure at the bottom is if you manage to shoe those two horses."

Looking at the total on the bill Joshua's eyes opened with amazement. It seemed to be an incredible amount of money. He folded the parchment carefully and put it in his pocket. Then he smiled at Rachel.

"Sara it's time for us to eat. Come."

He picked up the sack that Anna had just given to him and walked to the end of the stable where his stall was. Carefully he laid out the sacks contents on the box. They had a large wedge of bread, some cheese, and a leg of roasted lamb. The mug of water was still on the box from last night.

"Please sit down and eat with me Rachel", He said.

She hesitated. He could tell that she was worried about something

"I can't," she said.

"Why not"?

"Because this is your food Joshua You are the man and you must eat. There is only enough for you."

"Little John is coming back with food from the inn Rachel, this is for you."

Sasha barked and wagged his tail as Little John walked into the barn with two sacks of food. He began unloading them onto the box. There were bread rolls dipped in honey and two bowls with goat's milk and oats. Little John's and Rachel's eyes were both wide with astonishment.

"Well", said Joshua," what are we waiting for? Help yourself."

He could tell by the way their hands shook that they were ravenously hungry. Joshua ate sparingly. He wanted his guests to eat their fill. He declined to eat his bowl of oatmeal saying he was full. Rachel smiled at him.

"I know you're lying Joshua," she said. Then she asked "Can I save some of this for little James please?"

"Of course" said Joshua.

"Oh Mama this bread and honey is so good." Little John said. Rachel's' eyes filled with tears.

"How can we ever thank you Joshua?"

"You already have." He said. "But now I have to get back to work, I have two horses to shoe."

He was eager to show off his blacksmithing skills to the beautiful Rachel.

"While you are doing that Joshua, John and I will finish cleaning and bedding the horses."

Joshua was once again astonished that this nice girl would assist him in the hard work of grooming the animals. He did not think a woman should be doing such dirty heavy work; but he was delighted, as there was too much work for him and Little John to do by mid-day. He nodded to Rachel who immediately got the pitchfork and wheelbarrow.

While Little John and Rachel worked at cleaning the last few stalls, Joshua set about shoeing the horses. As he finished nailing the last shoe on the big stallions rear hoof, he looked up to see Rachel staring at him with admiration. His heart began to swell with pride.

"Aren't you scared of him?" she asked pointing at the horse

"I used to be" he said "but you have to talk to a horse and let him know you won't hurt him, and that you know what you are doing."

"Ruth says that we have run out of feed for the horses. If you like, John and I could go with the pony and fetch it."

Joshua shook his head.

Unfortunately I don't have enough money to buy feed," he said.

"That's all right. Ruth said to let them know that she will pay later in the week and they will let us have one or two bags for today."

Joshua was relieved to hear this. He had been worried that the horses would go hungry again.

"Do you know where to go for the feed"?

"Yes it's at Ephron's farm, just over the hill."

Joshua, still mindful of the beating he got from the robbers a couple of weeks previously, shook his head. The thought of Rachel and Little John being attacked by robbers, filled him with horror.

"I think I should go with you," he said.

"No Joshua. You have to run the business here. We will be fine."

Sasha barked and wagged his tail.

"Can we take Sasha with us Joshua?" Little John asked.

Sasha barked and wagged his tail again. Joshua laughed. He knew they would be safe with Sasha.

"Sure" he said, tying two large sacks for feed on the pony.

"Can I ride him Mama?" Little John's eyes danced with excitement.

Joshua nodded

"Sure you can, you can ride him with your mama."

Rachel shook her head.

"No Joshua, I'd rather walk, but John can ride."

Joshua lifted the little boy onto the pony's back and showed him where to hang onto the pony's mane. Then Rachel took the rope and led the pony out of the barn. Sasha suddenly let out a long low growl and bared his teeth. He was staring up the hill. A solitary figure was coming down the center of the dusty main street from the direction of the inn. Joshua saw that it was a Roman legionary. Sasha continued to growl. For some reason Joshua knew it was important for Rachel and John and Sasha to get going before the Roman arrived.

"Go Rachel go." he said, slapping the pony's haunch.

They took off walking away very fast away from the barn and the approaching soldier.

Chapter 25

Joshua felt his stomach tighten as the Roman approached. He looked such an intimidating figure with his armor chinking and his big broad sword swinging from his belt. Suddenly the index finger on Joshua's right hand began tingling. He remembered the Baby Kings little hand entwined around his finger. He felt a great calmness, a sensation of strength and confidence. He lifted his hand to his lips and kissed it, imagining the Baby's hand holding his. Then, turning to Sasha, who was still growling, he patted the dog.

"It's all right Sasha. Be quiet."

The Roman came up to Joshua. He had a scowl on his face and sweat on his forehead.

"I've come to inspect our horses."

Joshua studied the face in front of him. He had grey eyes and a large Roman nose. Strands of golden hair were sticking out from under his helmet. He was a rather young soldier. Joshua guessed him to be about five or six years older than himself. He probably could look quite handsome if he smiled Joshua thought. Behind those gray eyes, Joshua could sense a frightened little boy pretending to be a big man.

"Sure" Joshua smiled, "Come on in. By the way I am Joshua," he said holding out his hand.

The Roman took a step back. He was not used to such a show of friendliness and confidence. He considered the Jews to be whimpering, cowering dogs and he tended to treat them thus. This one however was different. He could not resist the sparkle and confidence in this young man's eyes. Gruffly he shook Joshua's hand.

"I am Captain Remus."

He followed Joshua into the barn and commenced examining his horses. He was obviously an accomplished horseman. He gently patted each horse's neck and stroked their foreheads speaking softly to them. He examined their teeth and their eyes. In each stall, he moved the straw bedding around with his foot checking to see if it was all fresh or just covering old bedding. By the time he had examined all ten horses he was smiling.

"These horses have been well tended." He said. "They have been fed, and watered and their bedding has been changed. Your fellow countrymen often half starve our animals, and charge us hugely. Have you got the bill?"

Joshua took the bill Ruth had written up and handed it to Captain Remus.

"You have charged for shoeing two horses. Can I see them?" the Roman said.

Joshua led him to first one and then the second horse he had shod that morning. The Roman picked up the back hooves and inspected them.

"A really good job Joshua. Who is the blacksmith?"

"I am." Joshua said feeling very proud.

The Roman looked at him in surprise.

"You look so young."

"Not much younger then yourself Captain."

The Roman laughed at the impudent young Jew whom he really could not help liking.

"You run a really good stable and blacksmiths shop." He said pulling out his pouch.

"Have you got a small sack or money belt?"

Joshua picked up a small sack from one of the stalls. The Roman began counting coins and dropping them into the sack. It seemed to take forever. When he was finished, he took a large gold coin out of his pouch.

"I would like to give you this extra for taking such good care of my horse Franko. He was quite sick when I left him here but he looks quite healthy now. My men will be here at sun up tomorrow for their horses, but I would like to take mine now. I will bring him back at sunset tonight."

"Thank you Captain. That will be fine."

He then led the animal out of his stall for the Roman. Captain Remus mounted his horse and, with a wave to Joshua, rode off.

Joshua carried the heavy sack of coins to Ruth's house and spilled them out on the table. Rachel's infant son, James, was on the floor banging a stick on the ground. Ruth was sitting on a stool watching him.

"They never pay the whole bill." she said shaking her head. "They always quibble and haggle and say we haven't fed their horses. They even once accused my husband of poisoning the animals. I have never known them pay more than half of what we ask," she said in astonishment. She counted out half the coins and the gold coin and handed them to Joshua.

"There you are my kind man, for your services. I would give you more but I have to pay for the feed we got from Ephron's farm. Perhaps tomorrow you or Rachel could take it and pay him?" Joshua shook his head.

"I can't take all this money from you Ruth. You already paid me a lot of money yesterday."

"Yes" she said with a smile, "and you gave that all away to Rachel. Joshua you have done two-weeks work in the last two days and I got twice as much as I would have expected. Besides which, if you had not come I am sure those two horses would have died. If that had happened I would have been lucky if those Romans hadn't burnt my house down with me in it."

"They are leaving tomorrow before dawn," Joshua said.

"And good riddance" Ruth muttered.

"Now, now, Ruth," said Joshua shaking his head, "they did pay us handsomely."

"I know, I know," she said, as she looked over her shoulder to make sure they were alone.

"I just wish they would have stayed in their own country and left us to ourselves."

"After they have gone, I don't suppose there will be much work to do in the forge," he said.

"Oh, there is always a farmer who wants a hoe or a rake or a plough fixing" She looked up at him. You will come and open up every day I hope?"

"Of course I will."

"I won't to be able to pay you as much, but I will split all the profit fifty-fifty," she said.

Joshua nodded. He was actually quite pleased that after the Romans left he would have so much less work to do. Although he enjoyed hard work, he had found the last week exhausting and now it was almost noon and the horses had to be fed and watered. He told Ruth he had to go. As he stepped out into the bright sunlight, he heard a bark. In the distance, he saw Rachel walking the pony, with Little John riding, and Sasha running alongside. When Sasha saw him, he left Rachel's side and came charging towards Joshua, his tail wagging, and jumped all over Joshua.

"Fine guard dog you are. You are supposed to stay at Rachel's side until they get here."

He walked over to the barn to wait for Rachel and Little John. To his surprise, a big man with a black beard was standing just inside the door of the barn. Sasha let out a low throaty growl.

"Hush now,". He said. "It's all right Sasha"

He turned to the man who had his hand on the handle of a large plough. The wood was split and the beam had broken away.

"Can I help you?" asked Joshua.

The man nodded towards the plough

"It hit a rock and broke" he said. "Can you fix it?"

Joshua bent down and began to study the broken plough. The beam had split and splintered around the blade. Without waiting for an answer, the man turned away.

"I will return on Friday."

As he exited the barn, he almost collided with Rachel and the pony.

"Hello Tiras," she said.

He nodded to her as he walked over to his ox, which he had left standing around the corner of the barn, and led him away.

"I got the feed Joshua," Rachel said.

Joshua nodded as he lifted Little John off the pony's back.

"What's wrong Joshua," she said, "You seem troubled"?

"I'm not sure I can fix that man's plough. The wood is all splintered. I think it is oak and I'm not a carpenter."

"Oh" said Rachel. She thought for a moment. "It's a pity you don't know a carpenter who could help you."

"That's it." he exclaimed. "Joseph will help me, I'm sure"

"Who is Joseph"?

"He is Mary's husband. They're living in my stable."

"Your stable"? Rachel looked even more confused.

Joshua laughed.

"Not my stable that I own. It's the stable that Jahleel lets me sleep in at the inn".

"Oh"

Rachel seemed even more bewildered as she untied the heavy feed sacks from the pony's back. Rachel like Ruth and many other residents of Bethlehem knew nothing at all about the wonderful Family that was living in the stable at the inn. Joshua wanted to tell her all about them. In fact, he wanted her to meet Mary and the Baby, but something stopped him from telling her. It was almost as if God wanted to keep the magic of this special Family a secret.

They began putting feed in all the horses' feedbags. When they had finished Rachel began tying a short rope to two empty pails, which she then placed across the pony's back.

"What are you doing Rachel"?

"I thought we could use the pony to help us fetch the water,"

She tied another two pails onto its back.

"What a brilliant idea Rachel" he shook his head "Why didn't I think of that"?

She smiled at him shyly as Little John picked up another empty pail.

"I'm helping too," he said.

Joshua looked around and found two more empty pails. Picking them up, he followed Rachel and her son out of the barn to the well. In no time at all with just two short trips to the well, they had watered all the horses. Just as they had finished watering the last horse and the pony, Ruth called out to them across the street. They looked at each other puzzled, shaking their heads. Together with Little John and Sasha, they made their way across the road to the widow's little house. As they got to the doorway, the air was filled with the tantalizing smell of cooked meat. The widow Ruth was bending down taking a roast chicken off a spit over the fire.

"I thought you people might be hungry,"

She brought the chicken over to the table and put it down in the center. There was a large loaf of bread and some figs in a bowl on the table.

"The baby fell asleep a few minutes ago Rachel. I gave him some goat's milk."

Rachel looked at the food.

"Oh thank you Ruth," she said. "This is so kind of you.".

"Can we really eat real chicken mama?" Little John asked.

Ruth laughed and Rachel and Joshua smiled. Ruth carved strips of chicken and put them on the table. They all passed the loaf around breaking off chunks and picking up pieces of hot chicken. It tasted so good to the hungry workers. Little John looked as though he was in heaven. He could not remember when he had last eaten chicken.

"You know Rachel," Ruth said. "I never realized what a tough time you had as a widow, or well, you know, since you lost your husband, until I lost my own husband. Then Joshua came in to my life and helped me and I realized how we must all share and take care of each other, just like Joshua does."

As Rachel nodded in agreement, Joshua blushed; he did not know what to say. He wished he were at the stable with Mary. She never embarrassed him. She always made him feel comfortable. He stood up.

"I have to go to the inn now, and help Jahleel."

"Can I come with you Joshua?" Little John asked.

He grinned and rubbed the boys head.

"Not today Little John, but I will be back to see you before sunset."

"We will water the horses again later Joshua." Rachel said.

Words could not express how grateful he felt. Before Rachel and Little John had come into his life, the chores had seemed overwhelming and endless. But they had taken on so much of his load, that he felt he just could not thank them enough. He nodded gratefully towards her.

"See you soon," he said, as he went out the backdoor.

Shielding his eyes against the bright sun he looked down the hillside towards the creek, and then up towards his stable. It seemed to him that the beautiful stable was sparkling magically in the afternoon sunshine.

He whistled for Sasha who was lying on the main street. The dog came bounding up behind him and followed him as he made his way across the creek to his stable. He could not wait to see his stable and visit Mary, Joseph and the Baby. Maybe the Baby would hold his finger again.

As he approached the stable, Joseph came out.

"Hello Joshua" he said warmly. "You have come to take Mica and Samson on the water run?" Joshua nodded,

"Only if it is convenient and won't disturb Mary or the Baby," he said.

"Mary and the Baby have been expecting you. In fact I think the baby is missing you Joshua."

Joshua felt that he was joking, but it still sounded very nice.

"I am just going to the inn for some supplies," Joseph added, "I'll be back in a while Joshua."

He held the stable door open for Joshua. Mary smiled her gentle smile at him as he came in. It felt unbelievably good to see her. He felt as though he was coming home to where he had always belonged.

"There you are Joshua," she said. "I told our little Baby you were coming and He smiled."

Joshua dropped down on his knees beside the manger and once again looked into those two little sparkling eyes. Tears of joy rolled down his face, as he reached out his right hand and rubbed his little finger against the tiny little hand. The Baby's little hand clutched around his finger and once again, he felt a feeling of peace. Time seemed to stand still. He wanted this moment never to end. It was difficult to say how much time passed.

Then the Baby turned his head towards Mary and, letting go of Joshua's hand, made a cooing sound to His Mother. Mary laughed her enchanting musical laugh.

"I think he is telling me it is time for him to be fed; I suppose you want to take Mica and Samson for their walk to the well?"

Mica brayed "Hee-haw" and Samson nodded his head. Joshua and Mary both laughed. He went to Samson's head.

"Come-on Samson. Let's go."

The Ox slowly got to his feet and seemed to nod to the Baby as he backed out to the stable. Next Joshua slowly ushered Mica backwards out of the stable. He had just finished hitching the cart up to Samson when Jahleel appeared at the back door of the inn. He looked as though he had a black eye and there was a cut on his forehead. He also seemed to be very upset about something.

"Are you all right Jahleel?"

Jahleel sat down on the stoop with his head in his hands. He did not speak for a few minutes. Then he shook his head,

"At least Anna is safe now".

Why? What happened to Anna?"

Joshua's voice was full of concern. In a quiet voice, the innkeeper began to tell him, all the time glancing nervously over his shoulder, about what had happened during lunch at the inn. As Anna was passing a table, one of the Romans had reached out and grabbed her, pulling her onto his lap. He had then started to kiss her. Jahleel was both enraged and fearful. He ran behind the legionary and, pretending to trip, emptied a whole jug of wine down the legionary's back. The legionary jumped up, cursing, as Anna fell onto the floor. She got up quickly and ran to the kitchen. The legionary wheeled around, drawing his sword, and cursing at the innkeeper. He was just about to hit Jahleel with the side of his broad sword when someone barked an order. It was Captain Remus. He scolded the soldier in his own Roman tongue, then turned to the keeper and told him not to be so clumsy in future.

Jahleel felt that Anna might still be in danger, so a little later he had taken her to his brother's house, which was just outside of town, and told her to stay there for a few days. Joshua was relieved to hear that Anna was safe and well away from the Romans. Jahleel seemed a little better having told the story.

Together they harnessed the ox and set off with Sasha and Mica to fetch water.

It seemed to be no time at all before they had finished hauling water and were back at the inn, unhitching Samson.

Chapter 26

Joshua led the two animals back to the stable. Once again, Joseph had cleaned it out and put fresh bedding down. The Baby was sleeping peacefully.

"Sit down Joshua and tell us what you have been doing," Mary said.

He felt a little shy at first with Joseph sitting there. He was used to having Mary and the Baby all to himself.

"Well," he began, "the Roman captain came this morning to inspect the horses. He said he was very pleased and even gave me a reward for looking after his horse so well. He said they are all leaving tomorrow."

"That's great news," said Joseph. "Maybe we can move into the inn tomorrow"?

"Oh Joseph, But I love Joshua's' stable. It is so cozy and just think how sad Samson and Mica would be. You know how much the baby loves them. Can't we stay here Joseph"?

Joseph shook his head, smiling at Mary.

"It certainly is cozy with the animals," he paused, "And we probably have a lot more privacy here than we would at the inn. If this is what you want Mary, we'll stay here in the stable."

"Oh thank you Joseph". She said.

Joshua was ecstatic that they would continue living in his stable. He felt very honored.

"I imagine you will find the blacksmithing business a lot quieter after the Romans leave tomorrow Joshua," Joseph said.

Joshua suddenly remembered the plough that Tiras had asked him to fix. He told Joseph about it. He said he was not sure he knew how to fix the wooden part, which had splintered.

"Why don't I come with you and have a look at it?" Joseph asked.

"Oh would you? That would be great," Joshua said jumping up.

At that, the Baby stirred, blinked his bright little eyes and seemed to look straight at Joshua.

"I . . . I'm sorry I woke the Baby". He stammered.

"Oh that's all right" Mary laughed, "he sleeps a lot"

The Baby seemed to smile and waved his little fists in the air.

"I think he wants to go with you both and help fix the plough," she said.

"Oh could he?" Joshua asked, "I would take good care of him. honestly"

Mary could not help laughing at Joshua's earnest young face.

"I know you would take very good care of him Joshua," she said, "But he really is too little to go anywhere just yet."

I just miss him so very much every time I leave the stable," Joshua said, with tears in his eyes.

I know" Mary said and he knew that she did.

He nodded to Mary, turned and walked out. Joseph followed him. They walked in silence down the meadow, over the creek and up the little hill to the big barn. Joshua was thinking about the little Baby.

When they arrived at the barn, Little John and Rachel were busy watering and feeding the horses. Joshua introduced Joseph to them. They both nodded shyly to this tall stranger. Then Joshua showed him the broken plough

"How tall is Tiras"? Joseph asked.

"A little shorter than you are Joseph. Why?"

"Well," said Joseph, "this plough is made of oak. Now it is unlikely that we shall be able to find an oak plank, so we may have to make the handles a little shorter when we make a new joint where the wood is split. Do you have a saw Joshua"?

Joshua ran to the end of the barn where there was a saw hanging on a nail. He brought it back to Joseph.

"Now one more thing," he said. "I really could do with a chisel and a plane, but if you do not have those tools, I may be able to manage with a sharp axe." Joshua said that he would go and ask Ruth.

He returned a few minutes later with an axe and a sharpening stone. While Joseph made a clean cut around the broken sections of the plough, Joshua sharpened the axe. Within an hour, Joseph had fashioned a perfect joint from the two ends where the wood had broken, Joshua was fascinated to see how quickly and cleverly Joseph fashioned the joint, using only the sharpened axe. He was amazed at how beautifully the two ends of wood fitted perfectly together. Finally, the carpenter drove a nail through the new joint to hold it together. When he was finished, the plough looked good. It was a little shorter on the handles than it had been. However, given the farmers small size, Joseph did not think this would be a problem

"You are so clever with wood Joseph." he said.

"And I am sure you are equally clever at forging horseshoes Joshua".

"How much do you think I should charge Tiras for this repair Joseph?"

Joseph reckoned around two denari. Joshua took out his pouch so he could pay Joseph.

Oh no Joshua, I do not need payment for this. If you really want to pay, then please give the money to Rachel. She has two little children to feed."

Joshua was touched by Joseph's kindness and generosity.

And now," Joseph said, "we should be getting back to the inn. I hope you will join us in our meal again Joshua."

Joshua beamed with delight.

I would love that." he said. "First, let me tell Rachel and Little John.

He found Rachel in the end stall brushing down the pony. Little John was lying on a bale of straw asleep. Rachel had already fed all the horses and put down fresh bedding.

"I don't know how to thank you Rachel for all your work. Joseph asked me to give you this," he said, putting the coins into her hand.

Tears welled up in her eyes.

"I can't possibly take this" she said.

"Nonsense" Joshua closed her fingers over the coins "Without you and Little John helping, these animals would have starved to death and the widow Ruth and I would be in terrible trouble with the Romans," he said looking into her brown eyes. He felt so much love for her.

"Thank you Joshua", she said, her eyes sparkling. Then she reached out and hugged him.

He felt euphoric as he stepped out of the stall.

"I-I am just going back with Joseph to the inn," he stammered, "I will be back at sunset."

She nodded to him and smiled.

Joseph and Joshua did not speak as they made their way up the dusty main street to the stable. Joshua felt he was walking beside his father again Then he realized that his father was there in spirit with them both as they walked up the hill to the inn. He also knew his father was feeling very proud of him.

When they reached the stable, Joseph went in with Joshua and Sasha at his heels. He told Mary that Joshua was joining them for supper and that he was going to the inn to get the food. The Baby was sleeping in the manger. Joshua told Mary all about Josephs work on the plough and the wonderful repair he had made.

"Joseph is a great carpenter". Mary said.

They were quiet for a few moments, lost in the bliss of heavenly peace in the stable. Then Mary said something that made Joshua's heart freeze.

"I shall really miss this little town of Bethlehem," she said wistfully.

"You . . . you mean you're going to leave here?" he asked, his voice almost breaking.

It had not occurred to him that this special Family, the Family he had grown to love, would be moving on.

"Oh not for a week or two", she said, "Not until the Baby is a little bit bigger." Joshua thought about this for a little while in silence.

"Where will you go?"

"Well first, I would like to visit my sister Elizabeth who lives in Galilee. After that, I am not sure. We will probably settle in a town nearby. But it will have to be a town that does not have a carpenter."

"But, but . . . will I ever see you again?' he asked, tears coursing down his cheeks.

"Of course you will Joshua You will always be a very welcome visitor to our home, wherever that may be".

She reached out and stroked his curly hair. He felt somewhat reassured but his heart still ached at the thought that she would not always live in his little stable. He could not imagine life without them.

Joseph came in with their supper and they prayed, giving thanks to God. They ate heartily. They talked about the Roman soldiers departing in the morning. They all felt a sense of relief. There was a certain tension at the inn with all these heavily armed soldiers around. Joshua told them he would feel very relieved when the last soldier's horse had left the barn in the morning. He added that he should be getting back to the barn to make sure everything was in order.

Just as he stood up to leave, the Baby awoke and reached his little arms up towards Joshua. Joshua felt as though his heart melted. He sank to his knees beside the manger and stroked the Baby's little hand with his finger. The Baby's little hand clutched around his finger and tears of happiness coursed down his face. Suddenly his fears and anxieties about the Roman soldiers and their horses left him. He knew in his heart that everything was going to be all right. He wished he could stay here forever holding on to little hand that encircled his finger.

After what seemed like ages the Baby let go of his hand and made a little squealing sound.

"I think he is telling you that you need to go and tend to the horses." Mary said.

Joshua smiled at her. He felt so grateful to her and Joseph for sharing their beautiful little Son with him. He slowly backed out of the stable nodding to them. He did not trust himself to speak, he was so overcome.

Before he knew it, he was back at the blacksmiths shed. Rachel was not there and he felt a little disappointed. However as he walked down the length of the barn he could see that all the horses had been fed and watered. They looked healthy, clean and happy and there was fresh bedding in each stall. He marveled at all the backbreaking work that Rachel and Little John had done. As he was thinking these thoughts, Sasha barked loudly. He heard galloping hooves approaching. He went to the front of the barn. Captain Remus was dismounting from his horse. He nodded to Joshua as he handed him the reins.

"We will be here at sunrise for our horses Joshua."

Then, without another word, he turned on his heel and strode of up the main street. Joshua reached up and patted the horse's neck.

"Your master sure is a strange man," he said to the horse as he put him into the stall.

It was beginning to get dark. He went to his own little stall at the end of the barn. His bed had been tidied up, with Rachel's blankets folded neatly on top of it. He lay down feeling very contented.

Chapter 27

Joshua awoke to the sound of Sasha barking. The first light of dawn was filtering through the cracks in the barn wall facing him. He got up and went quickly to the front of the barn. As he swung the large door open, the chill morning air blew in. Down the Main Street, he could hear the tramping of feet and soon could make out the dim figures of soldiers approaching. Strangely, he felt no fear. In his heart, he was still feeling the Baby's hand wrapped around his finger and he felt very safe.

The Romans entered the shed singly and in pairs. Some nodded to him and others ignored him. They each went to their own horse. A voice behind him said "Hello Joshua." This was Captain Remus leading his horse out of the stall. Joshua had not noticed him come in.

"Captain." he said. "I hope you have enjoyed your stay in Bethlehem"

The Roman laughed.

"I cannot honestly say I enjoy being in this country of yours. It is so different from Rome. But I will say again that you run a very good business here, and I will see to it that my Centurion gets to know about it. You can be certain of much business from our army in the future Joshua."

Joshua nodded his thanks, blushing at the compliment, as the Roman mounted his horse. With a wave of his hand, the captain cantered to the front of his soldiers and led them at a brisk trot up the hill and out of Bethlehem.

The sun was just beginning to peek over the horizon as the last soldier disappeared over the hill. The place suddenly seemed very silent and the magic of Bethlehem returned.

Eyes fixed on his beautiful stable, Joshua made his way down the hill to the little creek. When he got to the bank of the creek, he took off his tunic and laid it on the ground under the tree. Sasha wagged his tail and lay down on the tunic, as Joshua entered the water to bathe. The water was refreshing and he thanked God for all the wonders he was experiencing. It felt so very good to be alive with the warm sunshine on his face on this beautiful morning.

Finally, he climbed out of the stream and pulled his tunic out from beneath Sasha. The dog thought this was a game, and with a growl, pounced on the tunic, grabbing it in his mouth, and tugging on it. Joshua laughed and tugged back hard.

"Give me my tunic," he said, "you rascal." But Sasha only dug his paws in and pulled fiercely back. Suddenly Joshua lost his footing and fell down the bank. As he tumbled down, he put his hands out to save himself and his right hand was slashed by something very sharp. A cry of pain escaped his lips. He looked down and saw blood pouring out of his hand . . . He bent down and plunged it into the cold water. It stung terribly. When he pulled it out, he saw that there was a deep gash on the side of his hand, extending up towards his little finger. He looked around to see what could have caused it. There, sticking out of the ground, beside the creek, was what appeared to be a rusty spearhead.

Sasha came over to him and began licking his bleeding hand. Joshua felt a little cross with the dog for what had happened.

"See this," he said crossly, "this is because you would not give me my tunic".

Sasha hung his head in shame. Joshua had never spoken to him unkindly before.

"It's OK," he said patting the dog's head.

He could not bear to see his furry friend downcast.

"You didn't mean any harm."

He gave his dog a hug. Sasha wagged his tail.

Painfully, Joshua stood up. He was a little worried. He had heard from his mother and father how a cut from rusty metal could be serious and sometimes fatal. He got back into the creek and bathed his hand, which was now throbbing. The water turned crimson as his hand continued to seep blood. He rubbed the cut vigoursly although the pain was nearly unbearable. He was determined to rinse out any poison that might be there from the rusty spearhead. After a few minutes of rubbing and bathing his hand, he began to feel very weak.

He climbed out of the creek and looked around for something to wrap over his bleeding hand. He picked up his tunic but was reluctant to use it, as he would have nothing to wear if it got full of blood. Then he noticed that the sleeve of his tunic was badly ripped, at the seam, from the tugging match with Sasha. With his good hand, he put the torn tunic over his shoulder, and trudged back up the hill towards the shed, leaving a trail of blood.

He felt sad. His only tunic was badly torn and his hand would not stop bleeding. He remembered his pebble and hoped he had not lost it when he was tugging his tunic away from Sasha. Then he recalled giving it to Mary for the Baby. Suddenly he thought of his stable and the little Baby. How he wished the Baby would hold his finger right now! Just the thought of this seemed to help immensely. The throbbing decreased and his hand did not seem to hurt quite as much, and he knew somehow that the problems, of his torn tunic and injured hand, would be solved.

He remembered how his father had once received a bad gash on his leg. It would not stop bleeding. Ben-Gideon had used a red-hot piece of metal from the fire to burn his flesh and stop the bleeding. Joshua remembered closing his eyes as his father had held the red-hot iron in a pair of tongs and brought it close to his flesh. He could still smell the burning flesh in his mind, as the hot metal singed the wound. He had been quite young at the time and had asked his father if it had hurt doing that. His father who was dripping with sweat, just nodded. Joshua had marveled at how brave his father was. He wondered now if he would be brave enough to do the same thing to himself.

On arrival at the shed, he immediately got the fire going. With great difficulty, he used one hand on the big bellows to blow the embers until they were white hot. Then he selected a small flat piece of iron and held it in the glowing embers with the tongs. As he watched the metal get hot, he was startled by a loud bark from Sasha. He looked up to see Rachel and Little John entering the shed. Rachel immediately saw the trail of blood leading to where Joshua was standing, and the big pool of blood at his feet. She rushed to him.

"What has happened?" she asked, taking hold of his dripping hand. He tried to blink back the tears that had started rolling down his cheeks.

"I—I cut myself," Joshua replied, "and it won't stop bleeding".

"What happened to your tunic?" she asked.

"It got torn"

"Come here "she said as, with her arm around his shoulders she gently led him to a bale of straw and made him sit down. Then she tore a piece off the bottom of her skirt and gently bound his hand

"John," she said, "run over to the widow Ruth and tell her I need some rags to put on Joshua's hand." John scampered off.

"Why are you working? Why did you light the fire?"

He told her that he had intended to cauterize the wound, as he had seen his father do. She was incredulous.

"You mean you were going to burn yourself?" she asked.

"It would not stop bleeding," he said with tears in his eyes.

She pulled him in towards her and held him. She patted his back. He began to feel very lightheaded but happy.

John returned with an armful of rags. Rachel wrapped more rags around his hand and then bound it tightly with one last long piece of rag. Little John looked mournfully up into Joshua's face.

"You're not going to die are you?" he asked.

Joshua managed a feeble grin.

"No, Little John, I'm not going to die."

"How did it happen?" Rachel asked.

Joshua told about his bathing in the creek and his tug of war with Sasha. Then his voice quivered again, as he blurted,

"My tunic got ruined"

Rachel s inspected the tear.

"Oh I think I can fix this. Maybe Ruth can help me."

She had no sooner said this than Ruth appeared at the doorway. She shuffled in with her cane, carrying a steaming bowl in her hand, which she gave to Rachel

"Here is some peppermint tea and honey for Joshua. Now give me his tunic. I will mend it." She said taking it from Rachel. "And you Little John, you come with me. We are going to find something for Joshua to wear while I mend this."

She wagged her finger at Joshua.

"Now you lie down young man, in your bed and drink your tea."

She peered at his bandaged hand before shaking her head and shuffling out with little John trailing behind her.

Joshua looked at Rachel. He was beginning to feel a little better.

"It's really not that bad."

"Yes it is," she said, her brown eyes full of concern. "You have lost a lot of blood. Now here, drink some tea".

He sipped the hot liquid from the bowl she held. It tasted good. He felt weak and very shaky.

"Was it rusty, the spear head that cut you?" she asked.

He nodded his head. A worried frown wrinkled her forehead.

"Oh dear, I wonder if we should get Ramallah to look at it."

"Who is Ramallah?"

"He is a healer who lives in the middle of town. People say he heals many sicknesses with his prayers and potions. You know, a cut from rusty metal can be very serious Joshua."

"I know, I rinsed it very well in the stream. It will be all right Rachel."

He tried to stand up but his legs felt weak and he fell back down on the bale of straw.

Little John came in carrying a large robe.

"Here Joshua, Ruth said you are to put this on and lie down and go to sleep." he said solemnly.

Joshua struggled into the big long robe, which must have belonged to Zacharia. It was obviously much too big for him. Rachel giggled, and he blushed with embarrassment.

"Oh, I'm sorry Joshua," she said, "but it is a little big for you. Come on, let me help you to your bed. You really must lie down and rest."

She pulled his good arm around her shoulder and, coaxing him to stand up, supported him, and led him slowly to his bed at the end of the shed. He suddenly felt very tired and closed his eyes. Within a minute, he had fallen asleep. Rachel sent Little John over to play at Ruth's house and sat down on the floor beside Joshua to watch over him. His sleep seemed very troubled and restless.

He awoke shortly after noon, and seeing Rachel sitting beside him, asked her what time it was.

"It's early afternoon," she said, handing him a bowl of water. He was so thirsty that he drank it all. Then he started to get up.

"Where are you going?"

"I have to go to my stable."

Rachel smiled, thinking he was hallucinating

"But this is your stable." she said.

"No. I mean the stable at the inn."

"Why Joshua?"

"Because Jahleel will need me."

"But you can't possibly fetch water with your injured hand."

Although his hand still throbbed with pain, he felt considerably better since his sleep. He patted her on the arm.

"Rachel, I have to help him. I promised him I would. I am a lot better. Please help me."

Little John came in carrying his tunic. With help from Rachel, he struggled out of the big robe and donned the tunic. Ruth had not only mended the tear but she had also washed and dried the tunic. It looked almost new.

"Can John and I come with you to help?" Rachel asked him.

"Thank you for your kind offer," he said, "but it would help me greatly if you both would stay here and take care of the business while I am gone.".

"Oh that reminds me. While you were sleeping, Tiras came and picked up his plough. He seemed very pleased with the repair and said he will return tomorrow morning and pay you."

Joshua nodded, delighted that she had already dealt with a customer.

"I must go now Rachel." he said.

"You really should rest today," she said shaking her head in concern.

"I promise you I will be fine."

With a wave of his good hand he took off. He felt considerably better since his sleep. He did not feel as dizzy or lightheaded, as before, although his hand was still painfully sore. He made his way around the back of the widow Ruth's house, keeping very quiet as he went. He hoped she would not see him. The last thing he needed now was an argument with her about having to do his job at the inn. As he approached his stable, it seemed to sparkle in the early afternoon sunshine. He tapped on the stable door and put his head in. Mary was just placing the Baby in the manger. There was no sign of Joseph.

"Come in Joshua," She smiled.

"Oh my! What has happened to your hand"?

"I fell this morning when I was playing with Sasha, and cut it on a rusty spear head . . ."

"Oh dear, it looks as though it bled a lot."

She reached out and took his bloody bandaged hand in hers. The Baby let out a large squeal. Mary smiled.

"I think he wants you to talk to him Joshua."

Joshua turned and looked into those exquisite blue eyes. He felt as he always did in the Baby's presence, overcome with love and happiness. He reached out to touch the Infant with his good hand. The baby kept hitting his hand with tiny fists.

"I think he wants to see your sore hand Joshua," Mary said.

"But it's all messy and bloody."

"That's all right." She said, "Just let him touch it"

He brought his injured hand close to the Baby. The tip of his little finger was poking through the bandages. The Baby reached up and caught the tip of Joshua's finger. Suddenly the painful throbbing in his hand ceased and a beautiful cool tingling sensation coursed through him. The Baby cooed softly and let go of his finger. It was amazing. His hand felt completely healed.

He tore the bloody bandages away with his teeth where Rachel had knotted the rags and unwrapped his hand. It was still crusted with old blood but there was no pain or tenderness at all. Nor was there even a sign of a scar where before there had been a huge gash.

Mary shook her head solemnly.

"Tell no one of this Joshua," she said.

He knew instinctively that what had happened to his hand was a miracle. He also knew that God and Mary wanted this kept secret. He picked the bloody bandages up and put them in his pocket. He looked at the Baby who suddenly appeared to be fast asleep. He felt an urge to pray and give thanks to God. He looked at Mary and saw she was doing just that with her head bowed and her eyes closed. Silently he joined her in prayerful thanks. Time seemed to stand still as it always did in this heavenly little stable.

Joseph entered the stable breaking the spell. He looked tired and disheveled.

"Jahleel asked me to fix the front door of the inn". He said to Mary. "It got broken last night when two soldiers had a fight."

Then he noticed Joshua.

"Oh, hello Joshua. Jahleel is not feeling well and wonders if you could fetch the water yourself today? He said one barrel would be plenty, as the Romans have left. I can help you if you would like."

"Thank you Joseph, but I am sure you need a rest after fixing that door. It will be very easy for me today, with only one barrel. But I would like you to help me lift he barrel off the cart when I return, if it's not too much trouble?"

"Of course I will. Just come and get me when you are ready."

With that Joseph sat down beside Mary.

Joshua backed Samson out of the stable. He hitched the cart with the empty water barrel to Samson and made his way down the street to the well. Little John saw him coming and rushed into the shed to tell his mother. Rachel came out and strode quickly towards him. He placed the first pail of water on the ground and slopped some water onto his hand to wash the dried blood off. Rachel came up and grabbed his hand. She looked at it in bewilderment

"Where is the cut?" she asked.

Joshua just grinned. He loved the way she held his hand.

"Oh it's better now," he said with a shrug.

Little John, standing beside his mother, peered closely at Joshua's hand.

"Can I see it Joshua?"

He bent down and showed his hand to the little boy. As he did so, he saw Ruth shuffling down the road towards him. He quickly stood up and started filling the barrel in the cart.

"What do you think you are doing young man?" She asked sternly.

"Just getting some water for the inn," he replied sheepishly.

"What about your hand?"

"Oh, it's better now".

He held it out for her to see. She squinted at his hand, shook her head and muttered "all that fuss over nothing" as she shuffled back to her house.

Rachel looked a little annoyed.

"That was not *nothing*, Joshua," she whispered. "I saw it. It was a terrible cut. I just don't understand how it healed so quickly."

"Oh, blacksmiths heal very quickly. It's all the working with hot fires and iron".

"Really?" She said a look of wonderment in her eyes as she slowly shook her head.

He loved the way her long black curls fell over her shoulders when she did this.

She helped him empty the last few pails of water into the large barrel on the cart.

"Guess what," she said excitedly. "Ruth is roasting another chicken for us."

She paused, a worried look on her face.

"You will be able to join us for our meal won't you?"

Joshua thought for a moment. He loved being with Rachel, but nothing in this world was as wonderful as sharing a meal in his stable with Mary and Joseph.

"Oh that would be nice, but I have to clean out the stable," he said.

"That's all right," she replied. "We will wait for you and eat when you return."

He did not know what to say, so he nodded bashfully. Then with a wave, he turned and led Samson back up the main street.

When he got back to the inn, he backed Samson and the heavy water barrel up to the stoop, just as a young servant boy came out the back door.

"Here, let me help you with that," the boy said.

Together they slid the heavy barrel onto the rear stoop. Then Joshua crept quietly into the stable. Joseph was sleeping on the straw beside Mary, who had the Baby on her lap. The Baby smiled as soon as He saw Joshua.

Joshua felt worried about waking up Joseph.

"I'll bring Samson back later. "he whispered.

"It's all right Joshua," Mary said. "You can bring him in now. Joseph won't mind".

Once again, Joseph had already cleaned out the animal's stalls and the stable smelled sweet and inviting. Joshua quietly led the ox into his stall. Joseph was still snoring peacefully. Samson lay down and chewed grains. Joshua felt he was intruding and began to back quietly out the door.

"Oh please stay with us awhile," Mary said.

So he happily sat down beside the Baby and told her all about his day, and how great his hand felt. He talked about Rachel, Little John, and Ruth. The Baby seemed to listen to every word. Joshua looked at him tenderly.

"He seems to understand everything I am saying" he said.

"Oh he is such a wise little Baby," Mary said with such a lovely smile and a faraway look in her eyes.

Joseph woke up and, rubbing his eyes, sat up.

"Hello Joshua. I must have dozed off. I do not know about you, but I am hungry! I am going to the inn to fetch some food for us. I hope you will join us?"

Joshua nodded happily. He felt a little guilty, however, knowing that Rachel and Ruth had made supper and were waiting for him, but oh, how he loved sharing a meal with Mary and Joseph. They treated him as though he was their older son. The meals were full of laughter, fun, and talk about the inn, and blacksmithing and carpentry. Joshua felt he was learning a great deal, just listening to Joseph. His father would have respected this wise and gentle man.

After a very pleasant supper, he regretfully excused himself and made his way over the meadow to Ruth's little house, where he sat down to another meal. Ruth had roasted a chicken and made some of her fresh baked bread.

"I'm glad you finally got here Joshua. I'm starving." Little John blurted.

They all laughed as the little boy began cramming food into his mouth. Joshua was not very hungry, but pretended to be so, as he ate some of Ruth's homemade bread.

"This is so delicious Ruth," he said.

She did not reply although she was obviously pleased at the compliment. After they had finished eating Joshua took Little John and Sasha outside to the meadow and threw sticks for Sasha to chase. Little John was delighted when a stick he threw up in the air was caught by Sasha. The dog then wagged his tail, brought the stick back to the little boy, and dropped it at his feet.

"I wish I had my own dog," Little John said wistfully.

"Maybe one day you will" Joshua said throwing the stick for Sasha.

Dusk came quickly, and when it got too dark too play anymore, they went back into Ruth's house. There they all said their goodnights, and then Joshua, and Sasha made their way over the street to the shed and their warm bed.

As Joshua lay down he began thinking about the miraculous healing of his hand and the bliss of being close to the precious Infant.

Chapter 28

The next week was one of the nicest that Joshua could ever remember having. His mornings were spent playing catch with Sasha and Little John, or sitting on a straw bale just outside the shed, talking to Rachel.

Most mornings Rachel would bring bread and honey for a morning snack, and occasionally he would do a small job for a customer, like mending a broken shovel or sharpening a scythe. The townsfolk were slowly getting to know this cheerful young blacksmith, and customers would often stay awhile and chat to him.

His afternoons, as always, were taken up fetching water for the inn. Then came his favorite time of day, when he would sit down in the stable with the Baby and Mary and sometimes Joseph. He ate supper every night with them. It was like being back home with his parents, only much, much better. They laughed and joked and entertained each others with many fascinating stories.

On some nights, he would have a second meal with Ruth and Rachel, never mentioning that he had already eaten. He knew it would upset Ruth.

His special relationship with Mary, Joseph and the Baby was a secret. It was so wonderful being so close to the family. It felt even more special because it was a secret.

Every night he would retire to his bed with Sasha, and he often dreamt that the Baby was holding his little finger. After these dreams, he would always awake to the new day full of hope and happiness. Life was indeed wonderful. He had Sasha, money in his pocket, a nice bed to sleep in, his dear friends Rachel and Little John and Ruth, his job as the village blacksmith, his job at the inn, and best of all, his stable and the Holy Family. What more could a young man possibly want?

Chapter 29

It was seven days later, and Joshua was contemplating going to the inn early to fetch water, when Sasha suddenly began barking. Looking out of the front of the shed, he saw three figures astride huge animals, coming along the road into Bethlehem. His eyes opened in astonishment. He had never seen such large animals. He wondered if they were camels. He had heard about camels when he was younger but had never seen one.

As the men riding these beasts drew level with the shed, they reined the animals in and came to a stop. One of the men shouted a strange word. Then a wondrous thing happened. The three huge animals sank down together on their front knees. Then they lowered their back legs so that they appeared to be lying down on their stomachs in the middle of the street.

The man on the lead animal dismounted and walked towards Joshua. He was a very tall man with a long beard and a blue and white turban around his head. The turban appeared to be lined with gold. He looked like a king. The man spoke in a language that Joshua did not understand, but then said one or two words in Hebrew. He said the word for water and pointed to his large animal lying in the street. Joshua nodded. He always kept three or four pails of water in the shed. He went in and brought one of them out. The other two men had dismounted from their animals and were talking quietly with one another. They looked very handsome and regal in their fine expensive robes

Joshua nervously approached the first animal with the water pails. Sasha started growling, and the beast looked at the dog and bared its teeth. Joshua stopped dead in his tracks. The tall stranger laughed, and

145

patting Joshua on the shoulder, took the pail from him and placed it on the ground in front of his camel. The beast immediately began thirstily drinking from the pail.

The smallest of the three men then approached Joshua. He wore a red robe with a white fur lining at the neck. On his head, he wore what appeared to be a small golden crown covered with jewels. He had merry crinkly eyes and a short white beard. All three men wore exquisitely fine robes. Joshua had never seen such fine garments in his life. He assumed that these three men were kings or princes and felt awed in their presence. The smallest of the three was a little taller than Joshua. He stopped in front of Joshua and bowed from the waist.

"Good day young man." he said in almost perfect Hebrew. "Could you please tell us the name of this village and if it has an inn where we could dine and sleep for the day?" He had very kind crinkly eyes and Joshua immediately took a liking to him. At the same time, he was more than a little in awe to be speaking to such a regal gentleman.

"The village is called Bethlehem; there is an inn down the street, near the end, on the left side. They have fine food there."

He wondered if he should address the man as Your Highness. The wise little man seemed to sense Joshua's discomfort.

"We are Magi." he said.

Joshua was not quite sure what magi meant but he assumed it was a foreign word for kings. After all only kings could be dressed in such finery.

"We have come a long way from foreign lands," the Magus continued. "We travel only at night and sleep during the day. Does this inn, you speak of, have a stable for our camels?"

"It has a very small stable, but it would not have room for your camels. You may leave them here, if you wish, and I will stable them for you, except . . . except I have, uh never had camels before and I'm not sure what . . ."

"That's all right," the kindly magus said. "If you will be good enough to stable them, I will return at noon and take them out to graze in the meadow. First, we will ride up to the inn and unload our belongings. Then I shall return here with them. I wonder if you would be kind enough to fetch some water for our two camels."

Joshua nodded and ran into the shed, returning with two pails full of water. Looking sternly at his dog, he said "No growling Sasha" The dog looked downcast and lay down with his head on his paws as he watched Joshua warily approach the camel. The camel eyed him suspiciously.

"My, but these are ferocious looking beasts" he thought as he placed the pails in front of the camels. In no time at all the pails were empty. It was as though they had sucked the full pails into their stomachs without pausing for breath.

"They sure were thirsty" he said. "Do they need some more?"

"Maybe later when I return," The magus replied, "But now we must go to the inn as we are tired and hungry. Do you wish us to pay now for the camels?"

"You can pay when you are leaving town. Will you be staying in Bethlehem long?"

The magus shook his head.

"No. We shall be leaving tonight at sundown."

Joshua was pleased to hear this. He was excited to be of service to these Kings and their camels but he was also apprehensive about caring for these ferocious looking beasts.

The magi very elegantly climbed onto their mounts. On command, the animals clambered upright. Their legs were so long that the magi's heads were at roof top level. They started to amble off up the street. Rachel was approaching the shed, her baby in her arms and Little John trailing behind. As the magi and their camels passed by, she hurriedly stepped into Ruth's doorway clutching her children to her. Little John's eyes were open wide with astonishment as he watched. People up and down the street came out of their doorways to behold this amazing sight.

Rachel was breathless as she came into the shed.

"Who on earth are they Joshua?"

"They are magi," he said knowledgably. "They have come from far distant lands on their camels."

"Where are they going?"

"They are off to our inn for a meal and then one of them is returning here with the camels. They have requested that I stable them here today." He said proudly.

"You mean you are going to look after those huge animals?" she asked, her eyes wide with astonishment.

"Yes," he said grinning proudly.

"I'm sure not going near them." Little John said.

Joshua laughed and bent down.

"Little John, how would you like to run off up to the inn and get us some hot honeyed rolls for breakfast," he said, handing some coins to the boy. "And then you can have another look at the magi and tell us what is happening up there at the inn."

Little John nodded, grinning, and took off like a flash. While he was gone, Rachel and Joshua talked excitedly about the strangers and what such important noblemen were doing in the little town of Bethlehem, so far away from their homelands.

"I wonder why they only travel at nighttime." Rachel said.

"Maybe camels see better in the dark." Joshua said as Ruth came into the shed and joined them.

"You can bet the whole town will be talking about them fellas," Ruth said. "I've never seen such fine robes in all my life."

Her eyes lit up when Joshua told her that the camels were going to be stabled here.

"We should charge them the same rate as we charged the Romans," she said. "In fact, no, I think we should charge them more. Those camels will sure eat and drink more than horses".

They talked about what would be a fair price to ask the magi for stabling the camels and went on to discuss what the townsfolk would make of this big event. Little John returned with the honey rolls and they sat down around a bale of straw and ate breakfast in silence. Then Joshua jumped up.

"We had better get some stalls ready for those camels." he said.

"Right." said Ruth and Rachel together.

Ruth took baby James and shuffled across the street to her house while Rachel and little John helped Joshua to spread fresh straw in three stalls. Within a few minutes, the stalls were ready for the camels.

When Sasha barked they went to the doorway and looked out. In the distance, the smallest magus was riding his camel and leading the other two behind him. All the townspeople were standing in their doorways gazing open mouthed. When he arrived at the shed doorway, the magus shouted a strange command. The three camels slowly knelt down on their front knees and then lowered their back legs until they were lying in the street. The magus dismounted, turned and bowed to Joshua.

"What a lovely king this is." he thought, 'I wish he were our king here in Galilee instead of that horrible Herod"

It was well known, that Herod had no time for the common folk who were his subjects. He would not speak with them, Joshua had heard, let alone bow to them respectfully like this wise magus was doing to Joshua. Joshua bowed back.

"Good day sir, I hope you dined well at the inn."

"We did indeed kind sir. And now if you are ready, I will help you stable our camels for the day."

Joshua led the way to the three stalls they had prepared. The magus shouted another command and the three camels rose slowly to their feet. One by one, the magus led them, by their reins to their stalls. The animals were so tall that they had to bow their heads as they came through the doorway. When they were each standing in a stall, the magus issued another command and the camels sank down onto their fresh bedding.

"Will they eat oatmeal or grains?" Joshua asked

"Oh they will not need feeding for a while," the magus said. "They will actually chew on food they have already digested in their stomachs. See?" he said, pointing.

Sure enough, the camels were all chewing contentedly on their cud.

"I will return this afternoon," the magus continued, "and take them to graze in the meadow over there," he said, pointing across the road.

"For now, all they will need is some water, and I can see you have already taken care of that."

He bowed to Joshua and strode back towards the inn. Joshua was a little disappointed, as he had wished to talk with the magus. He had so many questions for the king. He stood at the shed doorway watching the figure going up the street. Rachel and Little John came and joined him. They had been hiding at the other end of the shed.

"Wow" the boy said. "Is he really a King?"

"I think so." Joshua replied.

"I wonder what they are doing in Bethlehem". Rachel asked,

"Did he say Joshua"?

"No," Joshua said shaking his head, "But he will return this afternoon to take the camels over to the meadow to graze. I am sure he will tell me more then."

The morning passed very quickly with all the talk being about the magi. Bethlehem had never seen such a spectacle as these three noblemen and their strange looking beasts called camels. Were they truly kings? The shed had a flurry of visitors from the town and countryside, all asking if they could come in and look at the camels. There were many mothers with young children. They would stand and gape in awe at the huge animals lying in the straw, chewing their cud.

A few men folk also visited the shed. Some brought in a broken implement that needed repair. Others inquired about the cost of fixing an implement that they had left at home. It was obvious, however that they had really come to look at the camels and to talk to Joshua who had actually spoken to their owners. Joshua felt very important. Suddenly he was a star in Bethlehem. Everyone wanted to talk to him. The whole town was abuzz with gossip and curiosity about these exotic visitors.

It was late afternoon before things finally quieted down at the shed and the last visitors left. Joshua was more than a little worried that he was late for his water run. He knew Jahleel would be upset but he did not want to leave Rachel alone with the camels. In addition, he was especially looking forward to talking with the Magi. He reminded himself that Jahleel had forgotten to pay him this week. He also felt, given the importance of his new paying customers, that his first duty lay here. Therefore, he continued to wait. The sun, which had sunk low in the sky, was casting long shadows when Joshua spied the figure of the magus coming down the main street. Rachel and Little John scampered off to the rear of the shed and lay down behind some straw bales, where they could listen to Joshua talking to the nobleman.

The magus bowed gracefully to Joshua, who bowed back.

"I trust our camels have been no trouble?"

"None at all sir," Joshua said leading him to the stalls.

The magus gave a sharp loud command and the three camels all stood up. He then took their reins and led them out of the shed. He handed Joshua 1 set of reins.

"I wonder if you would be kind enough to lead this camel," he said, "and accompany us across to the meadow?"

Joshua nodded taking the camels reins. The animal towered above him. Sasha growled once but Joshua shot him a glare and shook his head and the dog obediently hung his head and fell into step, beside

Joshua, and behind the other two camels. Joshua could sense the eyes of all the villagers peering out doorways, as he crossed the street. Little John had run to the door of the shed to watch. Joshua turned and shouted to him.

"Run up to the inn John, and tell Jahleel that I will be coming to fetch the water in a little while."

Little John nodded and scampered up the street.

They turned the corner at Ruth's house and continued into the meadow.

As soon as the animals' feet touched the grass, they began grazing. The magus dropped the reins and, striding over to a tree stump, sat down. Joshua let go of his camel and followed the nobleman. He stood beside him.

"We seem to have caused quite a stir in your little town," the magus said, smiling.

"That's true."

"I suppose that people are wondering what three noblemen from distant lands are doing in this kingdom."

Joshua nodded his head.

"Well," said the magus, "we are following a star"

"Following a star?"

"Yes. We are on a mission from the Creator of the Universe.

He looked at Joshua closely.

"He has given us a bright star to follow at night".

The magus went silent and gazed off into the distance. He seemed to be looking at the sky above the stable.

"But why?" Joshua asked him.

The magus remained silent for a moment and Joshua was not sure he had heard him.

Then he said, "What is your name?"

Joshua"

"Well Joshua, God has sent a Savior to this earth. This Newborn will be the Savior of the entire world. God has asked us to come and pay homage to the Savior, His gift to the world. He has given us a bright star to guide us. We know we are very close to where this baby is born because the star is getting lower and lower in the sky. In fact last night it seemed to be shining right over Bethlehem."

Joshua's mouth fell open in amazement. He knew instinctively that they were looking for *his* stable and the little Baby he loved so dearly.

The magus saw the look on his face.

"Joshua," he said, "What is it?" Do you know where the Baby Savior is?"

Joshua nodded and tears started streaming down his face. He felt Gods presence and knew it was all right to share this wonderful secret with the magus. He was so overcome with emotion that he could not speak. He just kept nodding his head as tears continued to stream down his cheeks. The magus seemed to understand. He patted Joshua's shoulder

"You do know, don't you?" he said quietly. Then, "It's all right. You can tell me."

They sat in silence for a few minutes.

"The Baby is in the stable . . ." Joshua began.

"In the stable?" the magus asked in astonishment, looking over his shoulder across the street at the blacksmith's shed.

"No, no," Joshua said, "I mean the stable at the inn where you are staying."

He pointed down the meadow to the inn. The magus shook his head in bewilderment.

"God's Baby King in a stable?" he repeated, as though he could not believe his ears.

"Yes, yes," Joshua said excitely.

He then told the magus everything. He talked about Magda's prophecy after his father's death, how God had a special mission for him. He spoke about his journey to Bethlehem, after his mother's death, and getting the stable cleaned out and ready. He recalled Mary and Joseph's arrival, and how he had given up his home to them because there was no room at the inn. He told the magus about the birth of the Savior, the shepherds, the star. He went on to talk about Mary, Joseph, the Baby, and the magical night of the Baby's birth.

The magus listened intently with growing excitement.

"Yes, yes," he kept saying and nodding his head.

Then he stood up. "Come Joshua," he said, "show me your stable".

"What about the camels?"

"We will take them with us."

The magus walked over to the camels and, taking their reins, turned towards the road. Joshua took the third camel's reins from him and led his camel behind the other two. As they walked up the main street people came out to their doors again. Little children waved at them as they passed. Joshua grinned and waved back, feeling like a celebrity. As they drew closer to the inn, he wondered what Mary and Joseph would think of these kings in their flowing robes. He wondered how he would explain their wish to see the Baby. However, he knew in his heart it was all part of Gods divine plan and that the coming event would be a joyful one.

When they arrived at the inn, the magus again shouted his strange command to the camels who sank down on their knees, and lay down in the street, outside the front door of the inn . . . The magus strode into the inn to find his companions. Joshua slipped around the side of the inn and ran over to the stable. The door was open and as always, Joshua knocked gently.

"Come in Joshua."

"I expect you want to take Samson and Mica on the water run," Joseph said. "Aren't you a little late today?"

'Yes" Joshua said.

Then he blurted out the story about the magi who had come at God's command from distant kingdoms and followed a star all the way to Bethlehem to pay homage to the Baby. He said that he had told them about the Baby. He finished by saying,

"Is it all right if they come and visit you?"

Mary and Joseph nodded together. They looked awestruck.

"You say they are kings?"

"Yes and they're dressed in the finest robes you have ever seen and riding on camels."

Joseph shook his head in wonderment.

"Well Joshua," he said, "you had better take the animals on their water run to make room in here for our royal visitors."

With that, Joshua backed first Samson and then Mica out of the stable. He hitched up the cart to Samson and put the empty water barrel on the cart.

Chapter 30

The three magi appeared from around the side of the building. The smallest one bowed to Joshua.

"Take us to the Baby King please Joshua."

Joshua bowed back to him.

"Please follow me" he said, leading them over to the stable.

He knocked gently on the open door.

"Come in" Joseph called.

"The magi have come and would like to see the Baby."

The Baby was lying in the manger. His eyes seemed to twinkle when he saw Joshua. The three magi entered the stable, slowly, almost reverently and sank to their knees. One of them placed a beautiful little golden casket at the foot of the manger. Joshua glanced at the three men. He saw that they all had tears streaming down their cheeks. He saw the same looks of rapture and awe that he had beheld on the shepherds' faces, the night of the Baby's birth.

Time seemed to stand still. There are no words to describe the joy and peace they felt. Then Jahleel's loud voice broke the spell. Joshua slowly rose to his feet, wiped his eyes and nodded to everyone as he backed out of the stable. Jahleel was loading the second barrel onto the cart.

"There you are Joshua," he said, pushing a few coins into Joshua's hand. "I am sorry I forgot to pay you this week."

"Thank you Jahleel", Joshua said, pocketing the coins.

"I thought you might not come today. It's getting dark."

The sun was indeed sinking low in the sky and, as they made their way around the side of the inn, Sasha started to bark at the camels lying in the street.

"Can you believe it?" Jahleel said as he led Samson down the street. "These kings are looking for a newborn king here in Bethlehem.I told them we don't have any such thing in this town. I told them they need to go and visit with King Herod. They said they had already spoken to him, and that he knew nothing about a newborn king. I am sure there is no new king around these parts. After all, as the innkeeper I would know. I get visitors from all over to my inn. I get to hear everything. If you ask me, they're in the wrong country altogether."

Joshua smiled as he listened to Jahleel rambling on about the Magi. The realization suddenly hit him that he was one of a chosen few who shared the secret of the miraculous birth of the Savior. Here was this beautiful little stable, right beside a bustling inn full of visitors, and only Joshua, some shepherds and the magi had been chosen, to witness this wonderful event. He realized that God wanted this kept secret from the world at this time.

They reached the well and started filling the barrels. Darkness fell as they emptied the last pail onto the small barrel on the donkey's back.

Back at the stable the magi presented gifts to Mary and Joseph for the Baby. From the large chest they had brought in, they handed Joseph another golden casket. It was filled to the brim with golden coins. Next, they handed him a small box full of incense. Finally, they removed a jar of Myrrh from the chest and, bowing reverently, handed it to Mary.

"Please accept these gifts." they said. "This Baby is God's most precious gift to the whole world. We are honored to have been called here to witness."

Almost overcome with awe, Mary and Joseph just nodded. Then, all together, they silently gave thanks and praise to God. Finally, the magi rose from their knees and bowed to the Baby and to Mary and Joseph. The smallest of the three said solemnly

"We must take our leave now."

"Thank you for coming," said Joseph, "and for your wonderful gifts. Will you visit us again?" Joseph asked.

One of the magi shook his head sadly.

"Regretfully not." He said. "We would dearly love to spend the remainder of our days in your presence with the Christ child. However, we must return to our own lands. We must go home by a different route; for we have been warned by an angel of God not to return to King Herod. He must not know the whereabouts of you or the Baby."

Joseph was not sure he understood but he nodded his head politely. The three magi bowed again before the Baby and backed out of the stable. It was dark outside but the great star over the stable bathed them in a heavenly light. They were all overcome with awe, joy and peace as they gazed up at the beautiful bright star which had led them to this stable. They stood for a few moments, reluctant to leave. Finally, they moved towards the inn to collect their belongings and pack for their long journey home

Chapter 31

After Joshua and Jahleel finished unloading the water barrels, the innkeeper went back into the inn huffing and puffing. Just then the magi appeared around the side of the inn with their camels all loaded up.

"You are not leaving are you?" Joshua asked his favorite magus.

The magus nodded solemnly.

"Yes Joshua, sadly we must depart."

He looked at the stable again.

"We have seen the Baby King and we shall take him in our hearts for the rest of our lives."

Then he pulled out a large purse from beneath his robes.

"Here Joshua," he said, "This is your payment for taking care of our camels and for bringing us to your stable." He handed Joshua the purse, which felt very heavy.

"Thank you kindly sir," Joshua replied, "but this purse feels so heavy. I am sure you have paid me too much."

The magus smiled.

"No Joshua. This is your just reward from all three of us. We have much wealth. You have given God a great service and it is only right that you should share some of our wealth. And now," he concluded, "we must be off."

He turned towards his camel and then turned back to Joshua. His laid his hand gently on Joshua's shoulder and looked directly into his eyes.

"Joshua", he said, "There are some bad people in the world, who would harm this Baby."

Joshua's eyes opened wide with fear and astonishment. The magus nodded.

"You must keep this precious Baby's birth a secret." he said. "Do you understand?"

Joshua did not know what to say. The notion that anyone would do harm to the Baby was horrifying to him. But he nodded his head anyway. Then the three magi mounted their camels and gave a loud command. As Joshua watched, the beasts rose slowly to their feet and stood upright, towering above him.

"Goodbye Joshua," the magi said. They moved out of the courtyard around the corner of the inn and into the dark night.

Joshua suddenly felt very alone. He crept over to the stable door wondering if it was too late to visit. The door was closed, and he knew instinctively that the family was sleeping. He said a silent prayer of blessing for them. How he longed to go in and just sit with them. Suddenly he sensed their presence with him. It was amazing. It was as though sensing his loneliness; the Family's spirit had come outside and said "Come on Joshua, let's all go back to your shed"

Sasha nuzzled his hand and together they went down the meadow, across the creek and up the hill to his shed. Rachel was waiting for him in the shed. She handed him a bowl of sweet peppermint tea.

"It was hot when I brought it," she said, "but has gone cold now. I was beginning to get worried because you are so much later than usual."

Oh how Joshua loved this lady.

"Thank you Rachel," he said. "Where is Little John"?

"Ruth is taking care of him and James. I heard you were leading camels around this afternoon. Where are the camels anyway?"

He told her that the magi had left town.

"What?" she asked. "Left town? How can that be? The whole village is talking about them. Some people's relatives are coming from the countryside tomorrow to see the camels. They will be so disappointed. Where are they going? Why did they leave so suddenly?"

Joshua smiled at her. He thought for a moment.

"Well Rachel," he said, carefully choosing his words, "they are seeking a newborn king. They thought he might be here in Bethlehem but having spent a day here, they have continued their journey."

"Looking for a newborn king?"

"Prophets say he will be king of all Israel".

"How did they know about this king," she asked, "and why would they be looking for him here in Bethlehem?"

"Well Rachel, it is said that this newborn will be very special and important to the whole world."

"Maybe he will get rid of these Romans and their taxes." Rachel exclaimed.

Joshua smiled and shook his head. He loved the way her eyes flashed when she was angry. He stifled a yawn.

"Oh," she said, "you must be exhausted. I saw you fetching a lot of water today. Did Jahleel pay you? Did those magi pay their bill?"

"Yes, yes" Joshua said excitedly pulling out the large silk purse. He bent down and emptied the contents on the floor. There were twelve large gold coins. They both gasped in amazement. Joshua was not sure how much all this gold was worth but he guessed it represented about two or three years of hard work for a blacksmith.

Then he counted out the *denari* he had earned at the inn, and handed them to Rachel.

"Oh, no," she said. "I can't take all this."

He knew she had very little money left from last week.

"Rachel" he said, "you have two little children to feed and rent to pay and besides you have earned it."

"How?" she asked. "I have done little for you since the Romans have left. Besides, shouldn't some of this be for Ruth?"

"No" he said putting the gold coins back into the purse. He held the last one up. "This is for Ruth." He yawned again.

"Oh you are so tired Joshua. I must leave and let you sleep. But," she hesitated and looked at the coins in her hand. Tears came in her eyes. "I don't know how to thank you."

She suddenly stood on tiptoe and kissed him gently on the cheek, then turned and ran out of the shed. He felt his cheek where her lips had brushed. He felt ecstatic as he stood their reliving the feeling of her soft lips. After a while, he lay down on his bed of straw and snuggled close to Sasha and blew out his candle.

The dream came suddenly. A band of soldiers came galloping into Bethlehem. Swords drawn, they began banging on people doors with their swords drawn. "Where is the baby King?" they shouted. Joshua woke, up drenched in sweat, and lay there shaking. Why would anyone want to harm the Baby, the most beautiful, most wonderful Baby in the whole world? He pondered what the magi had said to him. He wondered if he should run up to the inn and warn the family. For the first time since coming to Bethlehem, he felt scared and anxious. Maybe my mind is playing tricks on me, he said to himself. He lay on his straw bed worrying, for what seemed like hours, until the first streaks of dawn came slanting in through the chinks in the wall. Finally, he got up, called Sasha, and together they went down to the stream.

The star still bathed his stable in a comforting light. He prayed that the family would be kept from all harm and felt Gods reassuring presence. He bathed in the cold water and, even though he knew that God would protect the Baby, he still felt a vague uneasiness, as though not everything was going to be all right. He picked up his tunic and dried himself. Even Sasha seemed a little depressed as they made their way back to the shed. When he got there, he found Little John trying to light the fire.

"Fantastic," Joshua said to the little fellow.

He bent down and showed him how to do it.Rachel came in a few minutes later with honey rolls she had baked herself.

They had no sooner finished breakfast when people began dropping in to talk. They were all coming for a look at the camels and were very disappointed to hear that the royal visitors had left town the night before. The morning passed by very quickly with all the chatter and gossip. As soon as it was noon, Joshua left and made his way up to the inn. He was looking forward to seeing the Holy Family. He still had a knawing, anxious feeling and knew it would not pass until he saw the Baby and Mary.

Chapter 32

When he got to the inn, Jahleel's wife told him that they would not need any water today because the magi had left and they had brought extra water yesterday. She told Joshua that Jahleel was not feeling well and was sick in bed. Then she made Joshua sit down and eat a hearty bowl of stew that she had just made. He had not realized how hungry he was. She talked away while he ate. She told him that Anna was coming home in a few days at the end of the week. He listened to her talking about Anna, but he found it hard to concentrate. He just wanted to visit the stable. After politely pretending to listen to her for a few more minutes, he was finally able to rise and tell her that he was going to clean out the stable.

"You know," she said, "that couple is still in there. Jahleel told the gentleman, that we had room here, now, at the inn, but he said that they preferred to stay in the stable. Can you believe it? And his wife is expecting a baby?"

At that, she turned and walked out of the kitchen, shaking her head.

Joshua smiled. He thought it amusing that the precious Child had been born just outside her back door and she did not know a thing about it.

He went over to the stable. The door was open and Joseph was standing just inside.

"Hello Joshua", he said "come in."

Just stepping over the threshold, Joshua felt such a rush of joy and relief. He had missed being here so much. All his fears and anxieties disappeared. Mary was seated on the little stool holding the Baby. She smiled her warm welcoming smile. It felt so good to be near her. He sat down on the floor and they talked about his day. Then he told them about his terrible dream of soldiers hunting for the baby. As he spoke, the Baby began making funny little squealing noises and waved his little arms.

Would you like to hold him Joshua?" Mary asked.

Joshua nodded in wonder. He had never held a little baby in his arms before. He sat with his back against a bale of straw and Mary placed the Baby in his arms. Tears rolled down his cheeks. The Baby cooed and reached out His tiny hand, touching Joshua's lips. Joshua thought about his dream again. He felt so protective holding this little infant. He suddenly knew that God would protect the Baby from all harm, and in the same instant, he knew that the Baby would have to go into hiding. There were some very bad people who wished to harm Him. He felt sad because he knew that he would not be able to see the Baby when He was gone. He also knew, as he held this precious little infant in his arms that this little Spirit would always watch over him

"What's His name?" Joshua asked, tears streaming down his face. As Mary spoke the Baby's name, the donkey brayed loudly, drowning out her words. Mary laughed.

I think Mica is trying to tell you." she said.

The Baby seemed startled by the loud noise and started to cry. Mary took him from Joshua's arms and rubbed the little black pebble on his fingers. He immediately stopped crying and seemed to smile.

"I suppose you want to take Mica and Samson for water Joshua?" Joseph asked.

"Actually Jahleel said they have enough for today since the magi have left, but I can help by cleaning the stable and putting down fresh bedding."

"That would be nice. We can it together."

They took both animals out into the sunshine and put them in the meadow to graze. Then he and Joseph cleaned out the stable and put down the fresh straw bedding. They worked quickly and well together, and it was not long before the stable was clean and filled with the smell of fresh straw. When the animals came back in, they looked contented and happy, as they gazed at the little Baby sleeping in the manger.

Joseph sat down beside the manger and Joshua sat at the other side. Joseph asked him some questions about his childhood. Before long, he was telling them his whole life story again, starting from his earliest memories of prayers with his father in the morning stream, and Fuzz, their donkey, and their trips twice a year to Bethlehem to get supplies. He talked about his BarMitzva and the goatskin blanket. Mary asked if it was the same goatskin that he had left in the manger for the Baby. He smiled and told her that it was. He went on to tell them how Fuzz had gone missing and, shortly afterwards, about his father's terrible accident and death. How he had gone to Magda and how she had predicted that God had a special mission for him. He talked about Seth and his mother's illness and death. Tears flowed down his cheeks as he remembered his parents' deaths. Mary came and knelt beside him and held him in her arms as he cried softly. He felt peaceful in her comforting presence, and realized that he had told no one about his life or his losses since he had left home. Like his father, he was a very private person, but it felt so good to have told Mary and Joseph his life story.

"What happened after your mother died?" Mary asked.

He told them of Seth's drunkenness and bullying and, of God's invitation to leave everything and come to the "big city of Bethlehem." Mary and Joseph both smiled.

"Why are you smiling?" Joshua asked.

Joseph explained that Bethlehem was not really such a big town.

"But it has an inn and a huge marketplace."

"Yes," said Joseph, "but there are many towns and cities much larger than Bethlehem. Jerusalem is huge. It has a huge temple with a sanctuary called the Holy of Holies. There are houses in Jerusalem that have an upstairs and people actually climb upstairs to go to bed." Joshua's eyes opened wide with astonishment. He had never imagined there could be any place larger than Bethlehem.

"Would you tell us about how you journeyed here to Bethlehem?" Joseph asked. So he told them about his long trek to Bethlehem, how he had been robbed of his money and his goatskin blanket, and how God had sent Sasha to save him and be his friend. Sasha barked and wagged his tail and they all laughed. He went on to tell them how Sasha had got his goatskin back and how he had become the helper at the inn. He talked about cleaning the stable out and getting it nice and cozy,

"And then you came" he said simply.

"Yes," said Mary, "and then we came to your lovely, cozy stable. And where did you sleep that first night Joshua?"

Joshua grinned at her

"I slept out by the creek in the meadow under a big tree with Sasha."

"Weren't you scared?"

"At first I was, a little, but then the stars came out and suddenly the night seemed magical,"

Joshua had a dreamy look on his face as did Mary and Joseph.

"Then I must have fallen asleep", he added. "I woke up hearing the shepherds talking as they crossed the stream."

Mary and Joseph nodded in wonderment. They had never heard the full story of the shepherds.

"The youngest one was saying how an angel had come to them as they were tending their sheep" Joshua said. "The Angel told them how a Savior had been born. The Angel had said they would find Him in a stable in a manger" He paused,

"I knew then that I was to bring them here to see the new born Baby."

Mary and Joseph nodded again.

"We were so pleased to share our joy and happiness with you and the shepherds" Mary said. "I had just said to Joseph "if only we could share this with the whole world, and then suddenly you appeared with the shepherds."

Joshua smiled and sighed.

"That was the most special night ever."

They all nodded. It was so wonderful reliving that magical night of the little Saviors birth.

After a little while Joshua spoke again.

"I have never seen an angel. I wonder what they would look like."

"The one who came to me was a very beautiful person." Joseph said.

"An angel came to you?" Joshua said in astonishment.

"Yes"

"When, and what happened?" Joshua asked breathlessly.

"Many months ago one came to me in my sleep and spoke to me."

"How did you know it was an angel?"

"He told me he was a messenger from God."

As Joseph recounted this, his face was transfixed with happiness.

"The angel who appeared to me was truly wonderful," Mary said.

"You too, talked to an angel?" Joshua asked, his eyes lighting up with excitement.

Mary nodded and smiled, her beautiful smile, at the memory. They were all silent for a minute. Joseph stood up.

"I am going to get some food for our supper at the inn," he said.

As he walked out the door, Joshua looked up at Mary.

"Tell me about your angel please".

Mary smiled at him.

"Well," she said, "one day last year the Angel of the Lord visited me and spoke to me".

Her eyes took on a radiant dreamy look.

What did the angel say?"

Tears filled her eyes as she relived this memory.

"The angel appeared to me one night and said. "Hail Mary, full of grace, the Lord is with thee. Blessed art thou amongst women"

As Mary said these words, she appeared to be transfigured. Her whole being was illuminated, with a heavenly light, and for an instant, Joshua thought he glimpsed an angel standing beside her.

"I thought I saw your angel for a moment." he whispered.

"I feel the angel very close to me whenever I repeat those words," she said.

As he knelt there at the foot of the manger, Joshua looked at the little Baby sleeping so peacefully on his goatskin. He wished that he could stay in this place and in this state of grace for the rest of all eternity. Sadly, he realized that soon, like a beautiful meal, or any other joyful experience, that it had to end. And he suddenly felt very hungry. No sooner had the thought entered his head, than Joseph arrived back carrying a tray of food that smelled so good. He set the tray down on the straw bale. It was an amazing meal, roasted lamb with warm homemade bread, goats' milk, fresh figs and a carafe of wine.

As they ate, they talked about angels, who are God's messengers. They also talked about the shepherds and the magi and how God had guided them to the stable.

"Angels are so beautiful," Joshua said, "That's how you know they have been sent by God"

"That's right," Joseph answered, "And once you have seen an angel you never forget it and you always know that Angel will be there for you whenever you need God's help."

They talked softly, late into the night. Joshua yawned. He suddenly felt very tired and realized that he was keeping the family up very late. Just as he was taking leave and preparing to depart the Baby awoke. He bent down and looked into those little twinkling eyes. The Baby clutched his little finger and, as always, he felt enveloped by peace and love.

He had no memory of leaving the stable or of making his way back across the meadow to the shed. When he arrived, it was very dark. For once Rachel was not waiting for him. He figured it was so late that she had probably taken the children home to bed. He knew that she would have waited and worried about him, but his last visit at his stable was so full of wonder that he would not have missed it for anything in the world.

Chapter 33

B ack at the stable Mary and Joseph were in a deep sleep. Suddenly Joseph awoke. An angel was standing beside them. Joseph sat up and the Angel spoke quietly and urgently to him, telling him that the Baby was in grave danger. Gods' instructions were simple. Joseph was to wake Mary, take the Baby and flee to Egypt.

"When?" asked Joseph

"Immediately." The Angel said.

Knowing that Joseph would not know how to get to Egypt, the Angel told him not to worry, that he would be guided and protected all the way.

So, Joseph woke Mary and told her what the angel had said. On hearing that the Baby was in grave danger, Mary began to pack their few belongings. Within a few minutes they had the donkey saddled up and loaded. They petted Samson who looked mournfully at them. Then they backed Mica out of the stable.

"What about Joshua?" Mary asked.

"We shall pray and ask God to take care of him."

"But should we not stop and bid him goodbye?" she asked. "He will be so worried and upset."

"God has said we must not delay Mary. The Baby is in grave danger."

Mary nodded. She picked up the goatskin blanket that the Baby had slept on and held it close to her cheek and said a silent prayer. Then she laid it in a corner of the stall where she knew Joshua would find it.

With one last long tender look at the stable that had been their home for so many days, she went to the door and took the Baby from Joseph and held Him close to her heart. Just then, the donkey began braying and the Baby woke up and started to cry. Mary took Joshua's little black pebble out of her pocket and gently rubbed the Baby's fingers with it. The Baby clutched the little stone, and immediately stopped crying and cooed softly. She smiled and rocked him against her shoulder.

"Do we have everything Mary?" Joseph asked.

She looked around the stable one last time, sadly taking in every aspect of this beautiful cozy home that seemed to be blessed. As she did so, and unnoticed by her, the Baby gently dropped the pebble onto the straw at her feet. With a last sad look at the stable and a tender goodbye to Samson, they departed. She said a silent prayer for Joshua as they made their way up the dark main street, out of Bethlehem.

After a restless night, Joshua woke as dawn broke. He felt tired and uneasy. So he lay in his bed petting Sasha and thinking back to the previous evening. As he recalled his time in the stable, he began to feel happy and joyful again. He got up and ran with Sasha all the way to the creek where he bathed in the cold water and gave thanks for everything that had happened since he came to Bethlehem. He looked at his stable. There was no sign of the star this morning and this troubled him a little, but when he thought about it he realized that the sun had risen above the hill and was beginning to shine brightly.

When he got back to the shed Rachel was already there with some hot mint tea and bread rolls. They prayed and gave thanks and then shared the food together. After breakfast Joshua built Little John a swing at the back of the shed. Little John was enjoying being pushed on the swing when the first customer of the day arrived. A man called Reuben had brought a shovel with a broken handle and asked if Joshua could fix it.

Then he asked if Joshua had any camel dung. He had heard that camel dung was very good for helping figs to grow. Joshua explained that the camel dung had been put on the heap with all the other animals dung at the back of the shed. Reuben asked if the camel dung looked any different from the other animal dung.

"Not that I can recall" Joshua said laughing as he directed Reuben to the dung heap.

Then a farmer called Matthias appeared, smoking his pipe. He said that he had heard that "those three fellows on the camels" were spies from Egypt. He had heard that they were going to get their armies and come and fight the Romans. He asked Joshua if "those fellows" had asked him any questions about the Romans or the Roman army. Joshua had difficulty keeping a straight face as he solemnly told Matthias that they had asked no such questions, It amused Joshua to think that people were coming up with such incredible rumors about the magi's visit to Bethlehem. He spent a long time listening to Matthias's speculations. Finally the old man wandered off, still muttering about "those fellows on camels" as he puffed at his pipe.

The morning seemed to pass quickly and Joshua could hardly wait for midday to come. When the sun was overhead, Joshua set off across the meadow to the stable. But as he approached the stable it looked somehow different. The door was open wide. He put his head in. His heart sank. Except for the ox, the stable was bare. Samson looked so lonely and sad as he turned his head to Joshua. Joshua felt as though his heart had been wrenched out of his body. He had never felt such heartache before. Where were Mary and Joseph and the Baby? What had happened to them? Then he thought that maybe they had moved into the inn, although he knew that their donkey Mica, would still be in the stable if this were true. Nevertheless, he ran across the courtyard and in the back door of the inn. Jahleel's wife was in the kitchen stirring a pot of stew.

"Have you seen Mary and Joseph?" he asked her.

"Who?"

"Mary and Joseph, the couple in the stable?"

"Oh them? No. Come to think of it, the gentleman, Joseph you say? He usually comes in every morning for their breakfast. Such a nice man. But I didn't see him this morning."

She turned back to stirring the stew. Joshua left her and ran through the dining room and out onto the street. He looked up and down the main street desperately hoping for a glimpse of the family.

He knew they had gone. They had left Bethlehem forever. But his heart ached. He could not understand why. Why had they not come to say goodbye to him? What had happened? He wondered if something terrible had happened, but deep in his soul he knew they would be protected.

The ache in his heart was so great it reminded him of the day his father had died. With tears streaming down his face, he made his way around the side of the inn to the stable. He paused at the door and looked in again. Samson gazed mournfully at him. The stable looked so empty and bare that he could not stand looking at it. He turned and with his faithful friend Sasha trailing beside him he stumbled down the meadow to the big tree by the creek. Tears streaming down his face, he sat down with his back against the trunk. Sasha began licking his face. He put his arms around his furry friend and, burying his face in the dog's neck, wept uncontrollably.

It was there, hours later that Rachel found him. She came and knelt beside him.

"What is it Joshua?"

He raised his tearstained face to her.

"They've gone"

"Who? Who is gone?"

"Mary and Joseph." he said, his lips quivering.

"The couple you gave the stable to?"

He nodded.

Rachel was puzzled. She knew Joshua liked spending a lot of time at his stable with Mary and Joseph. He had mentioned them a few times, but she had no idea that they were so important to him.

"Why did they not tell you they were leaving?" she asked.

He shook his head.

"I don't know. Something must have happened," he said.

He began sobbing again. She pulled him close to her and with his head buried in her neck she stroked the back of his head. How she dearly loved this strong young man who had saved her and her children. She rocked him in her arms and let him cry.

When he had finally stopped crying she told him about her grief when her husband had disappeared. She said she had cried for weeks, and then one day, she had decided to go to the tree where they had first held hands and kissed. She had sat down close to the trunk and began to recall the happy memories.

"Suddenly," she said, "it was as though he was back there with me and then I knew he was safe and all right."

She gazed away and he could see the sadness in her wistful smile. Then she turned to him.

"Joshua maybe you should go and spend a little time in the stable. Lie down on the straw they slept on."

For the first time he felt a ray of hope. He realized he should go to the place he had felt so much happiness and peace during the last two weeks.

"You're right Rachel," he said rising to his feet. "Thank you."

He bent down and kissed her on the cheek, then turned and went up the meadow with Sasha. Rachel watched him walking into the distance. She waved but he did not turn around.

Chapter 34

When he reached the stable he stopped and knocked on the door before entering. His mind was so full of the happy memories he had in this stable that, for a moment, he forgot they were gone. He walked slowly into the empty stable and knelt before the empty manger. Tears started rolling down his cheeks again.

He spent a long time just kneeling in front of the empty manger. He looked all around the stable. Over in a corner he saw his goatskin blanket. He picked it up and held it against his face. He thought he could smell the Baby's fragrance. It felt so good just holding it against his face. How he would love to touch those little fingers just one more time. He began to cry softly again.

Suddenly Sasha barked loudly and Samson looked around. Sasha was digging in the straw near the doorway.

"What is it Sasha?" Joshua asked.

The dog continued to paw at the straw. Looking up at Joshua, let out another sharp bark and wagged his tail. Joshua got down and started groping in the straw. Then he found it: his black shiny pebble. As his hands closed around it, a wonderful peace enveloped him. He could feel the Baby's presence.

For a few minutes he stayed absolutely still, frightened that if he moved, he would break the spell. After what seemed a very long time he began to feel tired and hungry. He was reluctant to leave the stable however, so he lay down between Sasha and Samson, on his blanket and holding his precious pebble in his hand. He recalled his last visit. Was it only yesterday?. He remembered their talk about angels. It was not long before he was sleeping peacefully.

In a dream an angel came to him.

"Do not be afraid Joshua. The Holy Family is safe and well. God sent a messenger last night telling them that they were to depart immediately to escape a great danger. They had to flee at once and not delay. They are now safely on their way. Their love will always remain with you. And yes, Joshua, you will see them again."

Joshua woke up feeling a great sense of peace. He knew the family was safe and well. His pebble was still in his hand and he rolled it between his fingers. After another long time he rose to his feet and petted Samson, hugging and kissing the big beast who had shared so many wonderful moments with him.

Finally, he left the stable and strolled down the main street to his shed. Rachel met him at the door. She could see from his face that he had come to terms with his grief and seemed to be somehow stronger, more peaceful, wiser, and very handsome. She took his hand and together they crossed the street to Ruth's house.

They sat outside Ruth's back door. Ruth had laid a cloth down on the ground and they ate and drank and talked and laughed until darkness came. The stars came out and twinkled, lighting up the beautiful night sky over Bethlehem. They all sat in silence gazing up at the stars. There was a sense of sadness in the air, like the last day of summer, as though something precious was gone.

"I thought when those Romans left town I would be happy." Ruth said. "But somehow I feel worse than when they were here."

Rachel and Joshua just nodded. Even Little John seemed a little sad. He was sitting down with them, instead of running around and throwing sticks for Sasha to chase.

Eventually Ruth stood up and told them she was tired and going to bed. Rachel said that it was past little John's bedtime. Joshua stood up, stretched and looked wistfully across the meadow at his stable. The bright star had disappeared. Rachel saw the sadness on his face. She took his hand.

"I will get a lamp."

He looked into her lovely eyes and shook his head.

"Thank you Rachel, but I think I would like to sleep in my stable tonight."

She nodded thoughtfully.

"OK Joshua."

She watched him as he went down the meadow with Sasha He turned and waved to her just before he crossed the stream and then she lost sight of him as the darkness swallowed him up on the other side of the stream.

He felt a sense of anticipation as he approached the stable. Rolling the little pebble between his fingers, he walked faster and, once inside, sat down beside Samson. He knew the ox was happy to see him and he stroked the big beast lovingly.

It took him a few minutes for his eyes to adjust to the darkness. He picked up his goatskin blanket and lay down between Samson and Sasha, still holding his pebble warmly, in the palm of his hand. He felt the presence of the Holy Family. Then, he also sensed the presence of his father and mother, there, with him, in the stable. He knew they were very proud of him and happy to be here. He felt an overwhelming sense of peace and love. As he lay there in this blissful state, he thought of Magda and her words.

"Joshua, God loves you dearly, so much so, that he has a very special task for you and only you"

How he would love to talk again with that wise woman. As his eyes began to close, with his goatskin under his head, he held his black pebble in his hand and wrapped his other arm around Sasha's neck. "I wonder what God has planned for me now?" he thought, as he drifted off.

Summary of: JOSHUA'S STABLE

By Cathal O'Toole ...

Joshua's childhood is spent in a little hamlet, not far from Bethlehem. He loves helping his father, a blacksmith, in the forge. Twice a year they make an exciting two-day journey to Bethlahem, to get supplies.

Shortly after his fourteenth birthday, his father is fatally injured in a terrible accident. Joshua seeks comfort and counsel from Magda, the hamlet's wise old woman. She tells him that God has a special plan for him and him alone. She also foretells of some hardships in the days that lie ahead.

Within a month, he is orphaned as he struggles to keep the family's black-smiting business open, with the help of Seth, a lazy and dishonest employee. Seth however, sabotages all his efforts and Joshua turns to God for help. God tells him to *Come to Bethlehem.*

He sets off with some food, a little money, and his goatskin blanket. Arriving in Bethlehem, he finds work in the town's inn. He has to clean out the stable, and fetch water. In exchange for his services, he is allowed to live in the stable. He takes pride in his new home where he settles with the ox and Sasha, his dog.

When weary travelers Mary and Joseph arrive at the inn, they are told there is no room. Joshua proudly offers them "his" stable

Blessings and abundance flow into Joshua's life over the coming weeks.

About the author.

Cathal O'Toole attended Oxford University in England. He took up a career in social work. During childhood summers in Ireland on his aunt's farm, he spent many happy hours fetching water with the horse and cart and at the local village forge, watching the blacksmith at work.

He has five grown up children and currently lives in southern Ontario with his wife, Susan, youngest daughter, Katie, and two dogs, Hope and Molly. He loves swimming, fishing, reading, writing and traveling.